THE SNAKE FIEND

AND OTHER STORIES

BY
FARNSWORTH WRIGHT

Published by Bookship, 2023.

ISBN 978-1-915388-05-6

THE SNAKE FIEND

AND OTHER STORIES

BOOKSHIP

CONTENTS

THE FICTION OF FARNSWORTH WRIGHT

As editor of Weird Tales from 1924 to 1940 — arguably its Golden Age — Farnsworth Wright played a key role in the formation of modern fantasy and horror fiction. By providing the first professional market to accept works by Robert E Howard, C L Moore, Edmund Hamilton, Donald Wandrei and others, and by publishing the bulk of the work of H P Lovecraft and Clark Ashton Smith, Wright encouraged the writers who would shape the popular 20th century forms of what were then niche genres. (His influence wasn't only positive. Some of his editorial decisions, such as rejecting Lovecraft's *At the Mountains of Madness* and a number of Robert E Howard's stories, acted as significant discouragements.) This would be enough to make Wright a figure of some interest to fans and scholars of these fields. But he was also a writer himself, if far from prolific. And it is through his stories — most of which were published before he took up the editorship of Weird Tales — that we can get to know this key figure a little better. For, as with any writer, Farnsworth Wright's life informed his fiction.

Wright was born on the 29th July 1888 in Santa Barbara, California. His father, George Francis Wright, a graduate of the Naval Academy at Annapolis, was then working as a civil engineer. His mother, Genevieve Farnsworth, née Hard, had been trained as an operatic singer. George died in 1892 (when Farnsworth was only four), leaving Genevieve to support herself and her four children — oldest boy Fred, Farnsworth, youngest boy Paul Raymond and daughter Paula — by teaching music. The family moved to San Francisco, and were there for the devastating earthquake of 1906. Farnsworth then moved to Reno to attend the University of Nevada, and later attended the University of Washington in Seattle, working his way up to editorship of the campus's daily newspaper, and earning himself a BA in Journalism.

It was while attending the University of Nevada that he published his first fiction — not original works, but translations into Esperanto, the language invented by L L Zamenhof in 1887 as an attempt to bridge nationalistic gaps and, it was hoped, prevent future wars. Wright's translations into this new language included "The Tell-Tale Heart" by Edgar Allan Poe. A lifelong lover of poetry, he also translated verse by Longfellow, Blake, Eller Wheeler Wilcox, Robert Herrick and others. These appeared in the Esperanto periodicals Amerika Esperantisto and La Simbolo between 1910 and 1915. Wright would go on to teach the language, and the ideals behind it would be mentioned in one of his war stories, "The Vow".

In July 1913, Wright and his university roommate John P Rauen went bathing in the Pacific Ocean off Westport. Eddying currents around a deep, submerged hole took both into difficulties, and while Wright (who could not swim) managed to keep his head above the surface until rescued, Rauen (a good swimmer) drowned. His body was never recovered. This tragic and surely traumatic event would inform two of Wright's stories. The more inventive is the old-time diver's tussle with an octopus from "In the Depths", but "The Pole-Star", published in boys' magazine

The Open Road, is surely the closest to the real event, describing as it does a youthful swimming trip in which one member gets into serious difficulties. (Although neither story is supernatural, both have an air of the weird, thanks to the monstrous octopus of "In the Depths" and a fortune-teller's curse in "The Pole Star". The depiction of the constantly-relived nature of trauma in the former tale is insightful for its time.)

Wright's first job out of university was as a reporter for the Seattle Sun. He would go on to work on the reportorial staff of the Chicago Daily Tribune, and two of his early stories are about newspaper work. The already-mentioned "In the Depths" is about an unsuccessful cub reporter trying to hang onto his job through a last-chance assignment; "The Silent Shot", on the other hand, is about a more experienced reporter, one who sets about trying to solve a possible murder the police have seemingly overlooked. This tale is particularly notable for the forensic detail in which its protagonist examines a bullet wound to the victim's head — a far more gruesome passage than much of what would appear in Weird Tales. This raises the question of whether Wright ever saw such a wound firsthand. The level of detail makes it likely. But if he didn't during his time as a reporter, he certainly had ample opportunity in the next chapter of his life.

When the Second World War broke out, Wright was drafted as a private, but would find army work as a French interpreter, thanks to his facility with languages. Three of his stories are about the war, and all three engage in a debate about how it feels to be, on the one hand, part of one nation fighting another, and on the other hand, a human being faced with killing one's fellows. Wright's love of languages — and especially the potentially unifying Esperanto — gave him an initial sympathy with the people of other nations, and his trio of war stories, "Enemies", "The Vow", and "Lonesome Time", all touch to varying degrees on the connections between men who find themselves on opposing sides of a conflict.

After the war, Wright returned to working as a reporter (at first for the Hearst-owned Chicago Herald-Examiner), but also found work as a music critic. (He had in fact already been on the Chicago staff of Musical America before being drafted.) In addition, he worked as a press agent for the Chicago Grand Opera Association, and the Russian Grand Opera Company. Inevitably, music found its way into his fiction. "Out of the Frying Pan", a comic tale of a foreign opera singer whose inflated public image exceeds his income, has a knowing (and surely self-effacing) jab at opera promotors. "The Stolen Melody", perhaps the most lyrical of all of Wright's tales, reads less like a short story and more like an assertion of the value of artistry in the face of the often business-driven world of music. Another tale, the sentimental "Mother", displays some knowledge of the business-side of the backstage world, as well as its seedier elements. This story shows another, and somewhat surprising side of Wright, which will be dealt with a little later in this introduction.

Wright initially began work on the staff of Weird Tales as its chief submissions reader. It's at this point his own stories for "the Unique Magazine" began to be published. The earliest of these, the very short tales "The Closing Hand" and "The Teak-Wood Shrine", appeared under his own name, and today read like the work of a writer trying to pen the sort of thing that might appear in a magazine called Weird Tales. Neither is as sophisticated as the work of the magazine's greats — Lovecraft, Howard, Smith — and it's notable that of all the stories collected in the present volume, only one ("The Teak-Wood Shrine") actually features the supernatural with any degree of seriousness. (A third tale, "An Adventure in the Fourth Dimension", though chock-full of the fantastic, is clearly making fun of how nonsensical the weird can be.)

In 1924, Weird Tales was bought out by the Popular Fiction Publishing Company. Its then-editor Edwin Baird (who'd never had much interest in the weird, preferring the magazine's sister-title Detective Tales) was let go, and Wright was installed in his place. Wright would continue to publish fiction in the magazine but, doubtless wanting to avoid criticism for accepting his own work while rejecting others, did so under the pseudonym Francis Hard (obtained from his father's middle name and mother's maiden name, just as his own name came from his mother's middle name and father's surname).

These "Francis Hard" stories show a more polished approach to weird fiction than those that appeared under Wright's own name. They are longer than any of his earlier fiction, but also perhaps a little less personally revealing, unless we read something into their recurring themes. "Poisoned" is something of a *conte cruel*, a tale-with-a-twist made that little bit more confusing than it needs to be by having two protagonists with the same first name — or is Wright deliberately engaging with the theme of the double? "The Snake Fiend" is a more straightforward tale of human evil, but it's notable that both this story and "Poisoned" are driven by deep-seated jealousy over the love of a woman. (And it's worth, perhaps, contrasting these with the earlier, and far more gentle, tale of a man in search of love, "A Cookery Queen".)

Farnsworth Wright married in 1929. His bride, Marjorie Jeanette Zinkie, had known of him in their student days, thanks to his having dated a girlfriend of hers. It's clear from some of his early tales that Wright had a strongly romantic, and perhaps highly conservative, view of women, though perhaps one that was conventional for his time. Tales such as "The Medal of Virtue" and "Mother" are essentially moral fables about young women coming to the realization that they're straying from the correct path — a path that, in "Mother", precludes the wearing of tights and the singing of lewd songs. "Mother" was published in The Light, a periodical produced by the World's Purity Federation (their slogan: "The White Slave Traffic and Public Vice Can and Must Be Eliminated") — and is a surprising story considering Wright was the man who introduced the world to Margaret Brundage's Art Deco nudes, and used her scenes of woman-on-woman flagellation as covers to sell Weird Tales. Perhaps this was a hard-headed business decision, or perhaps it was down to marriage teaching him that such matters as the wearing of tights didn't necessarily mark a woman's first step on the road to moral turpitude.

Farnsworth and Marjorie celebrated the birth of their son, Robert Farnsworth, in 1930. This was also the year in which Wright took on the editorship of a second magazine, Oriental Tales (later relaunched as The Magic Carpet), a venue for adventurous and occasionally weird tales of the (to the bulk of its American readership) exotic lands of Asia, Asia Minor, the East Indies, and North and East Africa. Under his Francis Hard pseudonym, Wright published two of his own tales in this magazine, both substantially longer than anything he'd written previously. "The Picture of Judas" brings out the theme of the "moral double" — a namesake or other self at the opposite end of a moral spectrum — which can also be found in the "The Medal of Virtue" and perhaps in some of the early war tales. This story also features the mentally and morally destabilizing effect of sexual jealousy, as found in "Poisoned" and "The Snake Fiend". "The White Queen" is also about a dangerous rivalry for a woman's affections, and includes another of Wright's personal interests, the game of chess.

(There is one story by Wright not included in the current volume, "The Great Panjandrum", which originally appeared in Weird Tales in November 1924. Aside from the fact it's not a great story — it manages to suggest the potential for a number of interesting story twists while taking advantage of none of them — its extended use of racial stereotypes now make it far from the comic tale Wright evidently intended it to be.)

Wright's editorship of Weird Tales ended in 1940. By this point, working on the magazine had become impossible for him due to the effects of Parkinson's Disease, which he'd begun to experience two decades before. He quitted his position as editor in March 1940, and died only a short while later, on 12th June.

Wright's prose is occasionally notable for its evocation of mood or place, but generally has a functional directness no doubt picked up from his days as a jobbing reporter. His stories sometimes fail to develop their plots or drama as much as a modern reader might expect, but they do provide a window on the man who wrote them and his values, such as his belief in a potential brotherhood between all men of whatever nation, a romantic concern for the virtue of women, and a belief in the value of music and art.

Wright was also a poet. He used Weird Tales to bring some classic works before a readership that might not otherwise have been exposed to the likes of Keats, Walter Scott, Charles Kingsley, William Blake, Shakespeare, and Thomas Lovell Beddoes. (Likewise, he reprinted classic stories, helping to sketch out a canon of "the weird tale", including tales by Poe, Dickens, Hawthorne, de Maupassant, Pushkin, and others.) As well as Wright's fiction, this volume contains the few poems — those not in Esperanto — that he published, either under his own name or as Francis Hard, including two translations into English from German.

Farnsworth Wright's importance will continue to be his work as an editor in helping to shape the nascent fields of weird fiction, modern fantasy and horror, and his impact on the writers who worked in those genres. But it's to be hoped the present volume will provide a glimpse into another side of the man, and add something to our appreciation of Farnsworth Wright.

ENEMIES

The Overland Monthly, February 1917

Armand's baggy red trousers, dirty though they were after weeks of fighting, shone resplendent in the rays of the rising Belgian sun. The French uniforms worn during the first months of the Great War undoubtedly made a gorgeous show on parade, but they were excellent rifle targets—a fact which the French government had not yet learned.

Armand's rifle was slung carelessly over his shoulder. He walked slowly towards a well in a deserted farmyard. All the farms in that region were abandoned. The panic-stricken Belgian peasants, taking with them what household goods they could carry, were in wild flight westward towards Antwerp or northward into Holland.

Armand was tired and thirsty. He had a slight wound on the back of his hand, hardly more than a scratch, it is true, but very dirty, and needing to be washed and bound. He was alone, for he had become separated from his regiment a few hours before, during a night encounter with the Germans.

When the Great War broke out with the suddenness of an earthquake, Armand had nearly completed the military training which the French republic requires from each of its able-bodied citizens. But now he must continue to serve until peace should be declared, unless he should be killed or crippled before that time.

He had been hurried into Belgium with the first French troops sent to that unhappy country. Pressed northward by the onsweep of the German tidal wave, his company found itself attached to a Belgian regiment near the frontier of Holland, with the whole of Belgium lying between it and the armies of France. Now he was separated even from the Belgian troops.

Inexpressible hate for the invaders filled his breast. They were trying to murder his country. They had brought this unwelcome change into his life. Had it not been for this inexcusable war (Armand swelled with rage at the thought) he would now be back in his native village in southern France, there to take charge of his father's shop and live out the rest of his life in obscurity and peace.

One thing more. There was a not bad looking girl of his acquaintance in the village. She would make him an excellent wife. It was high time he was getting married, for would he not be master of his father's shop and thus be in business for himself? He was well able to support a wife, indeed, and this girl would not be bad! But now it could not be. The Germans—they were to blame for it all!

As Armand drew near the well a bullet hummed by him. He unslung his rifle at once, and looked around to locate his assailant. His first thought was that the farmhouse concealed a sniper, but the crack of the rifle did not come from that direction. Another bullet made him hastily seek what shelter he could find behind a large bush.

Cursing the French government for making living targets of its soldiers, he attentively examined the landscape to find his enemy. At length he caught sight of a spiked helmet peering from behind the trunk of a lone poplar, not more than four hundred yards away. He fired at once, but the helmet disappeared behind the tree trunk. Every time it appeared again, Armand fired, and each time the helmet was quickly withdrawn.

The German soldier who had made Armand the target for his fire at length hit on an expedient to outwit him. He carefully notched the tree with his knife. Then he placed his spiked helmet on his bayonet, and wedged the bayonet into the gash in the tree trunk. The helmet projected to one side, as if some one were trying to peer around the trunk.

Armand fired twice, and missed. Then the German leaped to the opposite side of the tree and fired three times before he retired behind the trunk again.

All morning the duel continued. Every few minutes the German sprang out to one side or the other from behind the tree and fired at Armand.

Armand returned the fire. But the tension irritated him almost beyond measure, and at times he could hardly see the sights on his rifle, so full of rage was he.

Who was this German? Why did he keep up this senseless fray? Why did he not decently come out and surrender, or at least go away? He must see that his shooting was accomplishing nothing! He had no business in this country anyway! He was a Boche, an invader, a tool of that accursed military despotism which so long had threatened France, and now had little Belgium back against the wall, fighting for life!

A bitter smile curled Armand's lips at the thought that the Boche was having equally as bad a time of it as he himself.

"The coward!" he thought. "He brought it on himself! To shoot at an unwarned man! No brave man would do such a thing. And he gave me no chance to defend myself!"

Then the thought intruded: "I would have done the same thing! If I had seen him first I would have shot, for this is war! But then he is a Boche! It is these red trousers that gave him his chance!"

Spitefully he blazed away at the German's helmet until he knocked it down. Then he felt quite satisfied with himself, as if he had shot the German instead of only his helmet. But when his enemy sprang out and fired again, Armand was beside himself with rage.

He was hungry and thirsty, and very angry. The wound in his hand was beginning to pain him. Already the sun was past its zenith.

He decided to stop this foolish fray, in which neither side was winning. He took from his pocket a large handkerchief, but at once put it back again. He wanted something white, but one would never suspect that his handkerchief had once been of that color. He opened his uniform and tore a large piece from his shirt. This he tied to his bayonet, to be a flag of parley. Fixing the bayonet to his rifle, he slowly waved the gun from side to side, and waited for the German to show himself.

When the enemy again leaped from behind the poplar he caught sight of Armand's improvised flag of truce and did not fire. Armand slowly advanced, waving the white flag.

As he approached the German, he groped in his memory for suitable German words in which to ask for an armistice. He had studied his enemy's language and even had written to correspondents in Germany before the war broke out.

The German held his rifle ready for use in case Armand should make any threatening move. But Armand, although burning with suppressed anger and indignation, had not come to kill. He wanted to eat and drink and wash his wounded hand.

"Qu'est ce que c'est?" the German called out as Armand

drew near.

"Sie sprechen Fransoesisch!" Armand exclaimed in astonishment.

"Yes, I speak French a little bit," the German answered slowly, in guttural French. "And you speak also my language, is it not so?"

"I have studied German a little," Armand replied in German. "But I never have talked it."

"This German may not be such a bad fellow, after all," he thought. "He speaks French, too! Still, he tried to kill me when my back was turned! I had best be on my guard."

Anger filled his heart.

He explained, in broken German, that he was tired of this shooting, and thought it might be well to declare an armistice until they had eaten and drunk and rested. The German willingly fell in with the scheme.

"Je ne veux pas vous—vous—toeten," he said.

So the two enemies suspended their strife and went together to the well. They shared each other's food and drank to each other's health, yet each hated the other in his heart.

"Prosit!" said Armand, lifting his cup of water.

"A votre sante!" replied the German.

Armand washed his wounded hand, and was about to bind it with his dirty handkerchief, but the German prevented him. He took from his knapsack a bandage. He sterilized Armand's wound, and bound the bandage tightly around the injured hand of his enemy.

Armand thanked him and asked him his name.

"Friedrich Krogoll," replied his enemy; "but my acquaintances all call me Fritz."

"Then I, too, will call you Fritz, Boche," said Armand. "I

am called Armand Roullier."

"Freue mich," said Fritz, relapsing into his own tongue. He extended his band, and Armand grasped it.

"I was afraid you might try to kiss me," laughed Fritz.

"Oh, I know where you get your idea of our customs," said Armand. "You have been visiting the cinema! A Frenchman doesn't exchange kisses with a stranger, especially if the stranger is a German."

And he thought: "This Boche is a good sport, even though he does murder our beautiful language. But he will bear watching."

"You come from Paris?" asked Fritz.

Each spoke in the language of the other, filling in the gaps in his vocabulary from his mother-tongue.

"No, I come from the south," said Armand. "And you?"

"From Munich. I am a Bavarian. But for two years now I am an instructor in the University at Goettingen. I teach entomology."

"So?" said Armand. "I never could go to the university. I had to work in my father's shop. My father is old, and I will manage the shop when I get back, if I escape being killed."

"Ah, this terrible slaughter!" said Fritz. "War is so terrible! The young men, they are the victims. No nation can spare its young men."

"That is fine talk for a German!" thought Armand. "Why did they begin this war if that is the way they feel?" But he did not say this aloud.

"Why are you not with your regiment?" asked Fritz, seating himself on the ground.

Armand explained how he had become separated from his comrades in arms.

"I got lost from my regiment because I was too deeply

interested in my profession," said Fritz. "In short, I was chasing a large night beetle. It flew several times, and each time I ran after it. It was not yet light, and I was behind our lines.

"Suddenly I heard the Belgians coming. They charged, yelling like all the devils of hell. They came between me and my command. I was afraid to fire, for fear I might hit my comrades. So I drew away, and thought only of how I could get back to my company. I went far back of the lines, out of the fighting, but it was darker than an Ethiopean Hades, and I did not go the right way. The firing stopped, and I walked a long distance trying to get back to my comrades. But when it was light, I found myself here. And the German soldiers—where are they? I don't know."

"I was one of the attacking party," said Armand. "How the fight turned out I don't know any more than you do. But—did you find that beetle?"

"Oh, no!" laughed Fritz. "I entirely forgot about the beetle when the Belgians charged. 'You and the Belgians,' I suppose I ought to say."

"What were you going to do with it?"

"The beetle? Oh, I was only curious. I could not be certain, in the dark, whether I had seen one like it before. I have a big collection of beetles at Goettingen, beetles from all over the world. Do insects interest you? Your fellow countryman, Fabre, has made a marvelous study of insect life."

"They don't interest me very much," said Armand. "I never collected them, not even butterflies. But I collect postage stamps and coins. It was to help my collecting that I studied German. I write to several collectors in your country, and I correspond regularly with a philatelist in

Munich. That is, we corresponded before the war. His name is Franz Link. Did you know him?”

“No. Munich is a large city, and, besides, I have not lived there for several years. My father sent me to Goettingen, where his brother is a professor of languages. There I did so well that I am now helping to teach in the entomology courses. It is a great study, entomology. But you should learn English, if you are a philatelist. In that language you can correspond all over the world—in Canada, India, the United States, Egypt, Africa and the islands of the Pacific Ocean. It must be very interesting, if one has the time to give to it. Tell me about your village. What is it like in that place?”

Armand told him all the interesting things he could think of about the village. “Professor” Fritz, as he dubbed the youthful looking assistant, then told long tales of the student life in his beloved Goettingen.

Each laughed at the other’s ridiculous errors of speech, for each was speaking a foreign tongue. In the absorbing interest of their conversation they took no note of the lapse of time.

“Hey, Professor Fritz,” Armand at last exclaimed, “I do believe the sun is about to set. It is time to eat again. Please give me some more of that delicious marmalade. And here is a big slice of that cheese you like so much. My father sent it to me out of his shop.”

“The marmalade was made by my mother in Munich,” said Fritz. “How she will laugh when I write her how I shared it with a Frenchman! Won’t she, though!”

He threw back his head and laughed heartily.

“How my father would rage if he knew his cheese was being eaten by a Boche! He had to send it by way of

England to get it to me."

Both laughed long and loudly. The German suddenly became very serious.

"Look!" he cried out. "The sun is setting! We must part."

"Yes," cried Armand. "We must part. Your way lies yonder. I must go west, but I don't know whether there are Germans between me and the Belgian troops. If there are, then I must go north."

"North!" cried Fritz. "That way lies Holland, and you can't get back until the war is over, if you cross the Dutch frontier."

"I must go west then," Armand replied. "The Dutch frontier is only four or five miles distant, for we have both come north since we left our regiments. And now, my friend"—his face became very grave—"I pray God we may never meet again while the war lasts. You are a good fellow, but we are enemies."

"Enemies?" exclaimed Fritz. "We *were* enemies. But now? Tell me, my friend, do you really want to shoot me?"

"I have already said," Armand answered with emotion, "that I pray God we may never meet again in this war. It would be murder. It would be like killing one's brother. It is a terrible thought."

Fritz stood in silence and listened to the distant roar of cannon. He thought of the lives that were being blotted out at the minute.

"Holland?" he said at last. "You say it is not far?"

"Not far," said Armand. "Six miles—perhaps—but maybe only three."

He saw his own thought reflected in the German's face.

"Allons, mon ami," said Fritz, after a minute of silence.

"Come!" said Armand.

They had been walking perhaps an hour, in silence, when they heard the pounding of hoofs. Through the deepening darkness they made out a troop of Belgian lancers, galloping west.

"Ha," said Armand to himself. "I am the master now. I will capture this fine fellow who was going to shoot me down without warning!"

But one look into his companion's smiling face shamed him from the unworthy attempt. He did not hail the cavalrymen, and they passed by in the dusk without seeing him.

The two continued north until they were stopped by a Dutch sentry. He could not converse with them, for he knew neither French nor German. An officer was called.

Armand explained that they had crossed the border into Holland to avoid having to shoot each other. The officer listened contemptuously, and sent them away under guard.

They were deserters, and their friends would call them traitors. Yet their minds were at peace, for a ray of light from that nobler age of which poets dream had fallen into their souls. So they smiled as they were led away.

The Dutch officer stood looking after them. Perhaps he was touched, perhaps he was only puzzled. At any rate, a mist came over his eyes, but it suddenly vanished, and he turned abruptly on his heel.

"Fools!" he muttered. "What would happen if all the soldiers should do that?"

THE VOW

The Overland Monthly, August 1917

A cold December rain was falling, but it was uncomfortably warm inside of the train that rolled slowly westward toward Liege. The gray haired, portly German who shared my compartment mopped his face with a handkerchief, rose and paced slowly back and forth. Then he abruptly resumed his seat, and stared out of the car window at the gently rolling fields, from which all traces of the great war had disappeared.

I had already studied him minutely. The nobility of his bearing attracted me, and something in his expression fascinated me. He seemed like one who had endured some terrible ordeal, which had impressed itself into his life and recorded itself indelibly on his face.

As if he felt my gaze, he suddenly looked up, and his eyes met mine. Abashed at being caught staring, I pulled from my pocket a newspaper and proceeded to peruse it, although I already had mastered its contents long before the German boarded the train at Aix-la-Chapelle.

The German noticed the newspaper, glanced at my face, and then looked at the paper again. All this I saw out of the corner of my eye.

"Pardon me, sir," he said, in a rich, sonorous voice, his accent only slightly suggesting his German origin. "I notice that you are reading the Chicago Tribune. May I ask whether you are an American?"

"Yes," I answered, thinking that he was probably a German who had lived in the United States.

"Your country fascinates me," he continued, "and I always enjoy talking to Americans, or to my fellow countrymen who have lived in America. It is the world's great melting pot, where peoples of different races and religions dwell in peace and amity together, animated by the same ideals, and co-operating one with another. The lesson of America will one day bring the International Republic."

I looked at him intently, trying to form a correct estimate of him. He was plainly an idealist, yet he seemed also a man who had lived through great experiences.

"So you are an internationalist," I remarked. "One meets them everywhere since the ending of the Great War."

"I was an internationalist even before the war," he said, somewhat proudly. "My belief in internationalism never faltered, even when the world was turned into a madhouse."

"Then you were not a soldier?" I suggested.

"I was a soldier despite my beliefs," he explained. "And yet my beliefs had much to do with my part in the war.

"I was with the first of the gray-clad legions that swept over this region. I took part in the first infantry charge against the cannon-battered forts of Liege, before the war became a siege-battle of trenches. But I went into battle without the spiritual exaltation that animated my comrades and made them glad to die for the Fatherland. My heart revolted at the part I was playing. It was not that my soul cried out against the wrong to little Belgium, for I would have felt the same way toward Russia or England or France. Before the forts of Liege I sought release from my soul-torment, but I bore a charmed life. Instead of death I received the Iron Cross for valor."

His face displayed a noble dignity such as I have seldom seen. His soft gray eyes seemed to fill with memories, to embrace the past and not the present in their field of vision. Even his fierce, stubby gray mustache could not frustrate the tenderness of those compassionate eyes.

"I fought through the war without receiving a scratch," he went on. "Once I nearly gained the death I coveted, but it was denied me. I brought my dearest friend into the grave instead."

"Some dear college chum?" I hazarded.

"Yes," he answered. "He laid down his life for me, and I am going now to visit his grave. He died in Flanders."

"You say you were friends in college," I said. "Was it at Heidelberg?"

"At Oxford," he replied.

"Then your dead comrade was an Englishman!" I exclaimed.

"No. He was a Frenchman."

"How on earth did you, a German, come to be the chum of a Frenchman in an English university? And how did you meet on the battlefield? As foes or as friends? By accident, or by tryst?"

"There were three of us," he explained. "One was an Englishman, one a Frenchman, and I was a German. We represented three diverse races, three dissimilar languages, yet no comrades ever loved each other more whole-heartedly than we three. We were true Corda Fratres, which is Latin for 'Brothers in Heart.'

"Filled with the spirit of internationalism and human brotherhood, we felt that our experience was but the forerunner of a similar feeling that some day would sweep over the world and break down the barriers of nationalism everywhere. So we met one night in my room and pledged ourselves to citizenship in the great World Commonwealth.

Gone for us, we declared, were the ties that bound us to our native countries. Henceforward we would live for no single nation, but for the world. I solemnly renounced my allegiance to Germany, and my comrades renounced their devotion to France and England. We failed to see that nationalism must be the basis for internationalism. A man does not renounce his family to become a member of his city or his country. He is at once a citizen of his nation and his district. If he is not a loyal member of his family, a good citizen of his town, he cannot truly be a citizen of his country. We failed to see that we must be true citizens of our nations to be citizens of the world. But I am digressing.

"We pledged ourselves never to bear arms for our individual countries, and we became citizens of the world brotherhood. We named Christmas Day, the anniversary of our vow, as a day of tryst, and agreed to renew our vow each year on that day. We signed the pledge with pens dipped in our own veins, as a token that the same blood flowed through us in spite of our different nationalities. We affixed our names according to the alphabetical order of the Esperanto names of our countries, Anglujo, Francujo and Germanujo: Harold William Hazelwood, Alfred Bonnet, Heinrich Schmid.

"The next summer saw us each in his own country. Then came the thunderclap. Europe speedily became a slaughter-house.

"A wave of patriotic fervor swept each country, and even those pacificists and socialists who had preached the general strike as a preventive of war rushed to the colors. Among them was Hazelwood, my English comrade, stricken by the enlistment fever which hit the English universities like a pestilence. He entered an English drill camp, and became a soldier of the king. Alfred Bonnet and I had no choice. We were receiving military training from our governments at that time, and were at once rushed to the front.

"The months that followed were like a nightmare. At first we advanced rapidly, overrunning Belgium and northern France like an onrushing tidal wave, by sheer force of men and guns. Village after village, city after city, fell to us without offering much resistance, except at Liege and Namur, where the Belgians made a heroic stand. Then the Battle of the Marne was fought, and the opposing armies dug themselves into the earth. The trench lines stretched from Switzerland to the North Sea.

"One day I was ordered to report to my general. I was at that time in Flanders.

"'Private Schmid,' said the general, 'I am informed that you speak both French and English like a native. Is it true?'

"'My pronunciation has been praised by natives of those two countries,' I replied.

"'Private Schmid,' the general continued, 'you have received the Iron Cross for valor. Your courage is unquestioned, and we wish to make further use of it. You will be fitted with a French uniform, given a name and full details regarding the French regiment to which you will belong. The man whose name you will bear is a prisoner in our hands, and he bears a close resemblance to you. You will seek out his regiment, impersonate the captured Henri Martel, and bring back certain information which we require. Report to me at midnight in your French uniform, when you will receive final instructions and be passed through our lines.'

"The assignment pleased me because of its very danger. There seemed but little chance to impersonate Henri

Martel successfully among those who knew him. I would cease to be an accredited murderer, for I would be put to death as a spy.

"I shaved off my mustache, got into the enemy's lines, it matters not how, and found Henri Martel's regiment. So little of it was left that it was joined to another command, and there remained only one or two men who had known Henri Martel. They did not discover the deception.

"I obtained the information that my general wanted, and then I was ready to escape. I hid my notes in my boots.

"It was Christmas Day. I was to go on sentry duty that night. I watched the great shells mount from the French guns behind me, and flit through the air with a dull whine, like foul bats, and now and then a German shell plopped into the ground near me. They made a hideous noise, plowing holes into the earth as if they wanted to get back to the infernal regions where they belonged. I watched the cannons spit fire. I heard an occasional dull roar, miles away to the north, from our huge German forty-twos, which the English soldiers called Jack Johnsons because of the clouds of black smoke which they belched. I had seen those monsters pounding Liege in the first days of the war, and I thought they must surely succeed in blasting a path to Calais and Paris, and even to Dover and London. Nothing seemed able to stand against them.

"My spirits sank lower and lower as my hour approached to go on sentry duty. At last the minute came. I received the countersign, and took my place in a sort of listening pit, with a telephone by my side to give a quick alarm in case of attack.

"I was preparing to make my flight, when through the communicating trench a small group approached, in command of a lieutenant. It was a party of newspaper correspondents. With them was an Englishman who had been wounded in the arm. He was acting as interpreter between the French and British soldiers, for his wound unfitted him for other military duty.

"I did not at first notice the young lieutenant, for my eyes were popping out of my head at sight of the interpreter. It was my English comrade, Hazelwood.

"He started when he saw me. Then he gazed intently into my face to assure himself that it was really I. He strove to conceal his recognition of me, so as not to doom me, but even his impassive English face could not become a mask after that unexpected meeting.

"The lieutenant addressed him, but Hazelwood did not hear. The lieutenant saw the direction of his gaze, and raised a flashlight to my face.

"'Heinrich!' he ejaculated, recoiling a pace.

"The lieutenant was Alfred Bonnet.

"'Alfred!' I exclaimed. 'It is you! And Harold is here, too! Do you remember? This is our trysting day! But I am discovered, and now I will find the death I have sought ever since I was forced to bear arms against my brothers. I am a German spy.

"'Oh, Heinrich, this is indeed the day of our tryst,' put in Hazelwood, in English. 'We swore eternal friendship, but in this tragic moment we are met as enemies!'

"'Wait for me in the communicating trench,' Bonnet ordered. 'I wish a few words with this German before I give him into custody.'

"The soldiers and correspondents withdrew, and Hazelwood went with them, leaving me alone with Bonnet.

"'Heinrich, I am desolated,' he exclaimed. 'I cannot let

you perish. Promise that you will never use against France any military information you have gained, and you shall escape.

"'Alfred,' I replied, 'I have violated all my ideals by fighting in this war, and I want to be allowed to die.'

"'Heinrich,' he replied with emotion, 'I cannot permit it. You must at once run for your lines. Go now, while there is yet time.

"At that he fired a shot into the air.

"'Now they are coming. Run, run quickly,' he entreated.

"I stood still, and then he shot himself in the shoulder.

"'Don't wait! I will say that you shot me in trying to escape. Oh, Heinrich, run, for God's sake, run!' he implored, in an agony of impatience.

"He sank to the ground, and I ran blindly into the night. The shots of my pursuers whistled after me. I stumbled into one of our barbed wire entanglements, and went through it, leaving much of my clothing on the wire.

"How I crawled through the remaining entanglements amid the hail of bullets is more than I can say. I passed the last barrier, then stood upright and walked slowly toward the German trenches. In the glare of the fire balloons my French uniform was recognized, and I became the target of German bullets. I suppose the men in the trenches thought the French were attacking. But I bore a charmed life, as at all times during the war, and I stumbled into a German trench in a faint, but without a wound.

"When I came to, I was lying in a field hospital. My boots were gone, and I knew that the information which they contained, and which Bonnet had asked me never to use against France, was even then before the general. I was congratulated for my work, and given a four weeks' furlough.

"Not until the war was ended did I learn what had become of Alfred Bonnet. He fell ill of his self-inflicted wound and of the excitement which my appearance and escape had caused him. In his delirium he called on me, pleading with me, implored and begged me to escape. Again and again he lived over his meeting with me, and exhorted me to run, run, and keep running.

"Out of his own mouth he was convicted of aiding an enemy spy to escape. He was tried and shot. On his grave was placed this inscription:

"*'Traitre   Il a perfide son pays.'*

"Hazelwood was wounded again shortly afterwards, and took part in the war no more. Bonnet, rotting in a traitor's grave, at least was at rest. Only I, the most ardent internationalist of the three, was doomed to fight on and on as a nationalist, until the very last day of the great conflict. I fought at Ypres, at Verdun, in Picardy, sometimes against the British and sometimes against the French. Several times my regiment was decimated, and I was assigned to new commands, but I always came through without a wound.

"When the war was over, my first thought was of Bonnet, and then I learned from Hazelwood how he had lost his life in saving mine.

"I am now on my way to Bonnet's grave in Flanders. Hazelwood and I have removed the lying epitaph which stigmatized our comrade as a traitor, and we have built him a worthy monument. Each year, on Christmas Day, we clasp hands over his grave and offer prayers for his soul.

"Last Christmas, after our tryst, I went with Hazelwood to England, but this year he will spend several quiet weeks with me in Aix.

"It is good to have such a comrade," he concluded, and smiled for the first time since he had been talking to me. The sadness of his face modified his smile, making of it a smile of consecration rather than one of gladness.

The train was rolling into Liege when he finished his narration, and I had to change for the express to Paris. I bade farewell to my new-found friend with genuine regret at parting from him so soon.

Three weeks later I was motoring through the war zone with a friend. We had been visiting the ruins at Ypres, and from there we turned southeast. A few miles west of the Belgian frontier my gasoline gave out.

While my friend waited in the car, I took a pail and went to the nearest farmhouse, walking through a line of trees that had been pollarded by shell-fire. I succeeded in getting a few gallons of gasoline, and started back with it, when I came across a grave with a marble headstone. I had seen so many soldiers' graves in the field that they no longer interested me. Possibly it was the marble headstone that caused me to stop, or perhaps it was the weight of the gasoline.

The headstone bore the name of Alfred Bonnet.

Reverently I removed my hat, and knelt down in the falling rain to read the epitaph. In three languages— English, French and German—was inscribed:

"A noble friend, a true patriot, he died a martyr to his country, which was the world. May his soul rest in peace."

LONESOME TIME

The Overland Monthly, October 1919

The sun poised like a glowing cannon ball on top of the ridge, and slowly began to sink as the last of the airplanes lighted gently, like a bird, on the plain. Allen, whose machine had been the first to land, looked on and admired the light build of the planes and the easy grace of the landings. These were fighting craft, the wasps of the sky, the smallest and the fleetest of the squadron. They had been engaged that afternoon in mimic warfare—rearing like horses, looping, rolling, tumbling, two miles above the ground, to keep in trim for the reality of actual combat.

Allen was in love with the graceful little biplanes in which he had been playing war behind the fighting line for the last two weeks. Measuring only thirteen feet from tip to tip of the wings, built lightly, fitted with sturdy liberty engines, they responded instantly to their pilot's touch, and were a welcome change from the large observation and bombing planes to which he was accustomed.

A swarm of mechanics and helpers ran the biplanes into the airdrome and commenced to overhaul them, while gunsmiths speedily dismounted the machine guns and began to clean them and make them ready for the next flight. The aviator that had just landed came over to Allen, and opened his cigarette case. Allen declined the proffered smoke, and the lieutenant passed on to the farther end of the shed, where a group of aviators were talking and laughing, and playing with a frolicsome spaniel that belonged to the squadron.

Allen did not join them, but sat alone, resting his chin on his hands. He was busy with his thoughts, and did not want his mood disturbed. The glowing disk of the sun disappeared, and the low crest of the ridge was sharply silhouetted against the western sky, with its little grove of shell torn trees standing out in relief like a wharf jutting into the water. Beyond that ridge was the Atlantic Ocean, and home. Allen heard only the laughter of his brother officers, the barking of the spaniel, and the distant irregular shouting of cannon. The sounds did not register on his consciousness. He heard them, but he did not notice them, for he was absorbed in his musings.

Allen did not need to feast his eyes on the little snapshot that he carried always with him, for the picture was graven on his memory. He saw Helen plainly in his mind's eyes, her long yellow hair cascading over her shoulders in bewitching disarray, her blue eyes dancing with light, her face radiant with sunshine. He pictured her countenance as he liked it best, brimming with love, and he lived over in happy retrospect the blissful vacation they had spent together, less than a year before. They had canoed and tramped much, and the acid test of spending a month almost constantly in each other's company had only made him love her even more devotedly than before. He had studied her moods, her expression, her every gesture, longing, doubting, carefully noting each little sign that perhaps she returned the love that filled his being.

It was at this same lonesome hour of the day, the restful period just after sunset, that he had found the courage to speak what was on his mind. Tonight there would be another big round moon, like the one that had made a long flashing lane across the lake to them that evening, as they drifted on in dreamy silence in the canoe, forgetting place, forgetting time, forgetting everything except that they loved each other.

Now he was a lieutenant in the aviation corps, fighting in France against his country's enemies. She was immensely proud of her big soldier boy, but he knew that she watched every mail in dread, lest it bring news that would break her heart. She had smiled bravely when she bade him good-bye at the railroad station, but the trembling of her lips showed the effort she was making to keep back her tears. She knew how eager he was to go, after he received his commission, and she was ready to make the sacrifice, if need be, for her country's good, but she dreaded to part from him lest he might never return.

To his mind, death was only an incident, a necessary risk, but not one to be weighed too gravely. But now he suddenly realized what it would mean to her. Most of the light and sweetness of life had gone when he went to France, for she loved him deeply.

He pictured her face at news of his death, and tried to realize the sickening catch at her heart, the growing sense of bereavement, the aching pain, the sleepless nights, the scalding tears, the void in her life that would never be entirely filled. The unutterable sadness of it so depressed him that he took out her picture, which he always kept nearest his heart, and gazed long into the laughing eyes of the photograph.

His mood was interrupted by an outcry. Warning had come of the approach of hostile airplanes. Allen rushed to his machine, thrilled with the realization that he was at last to experience actual combat in the sky. Several black dots showed high up in the east, and he knew that these were his antagonists.

Twenty American planes skimmed over the ground and began to climb, not in spirals, but directly upwards, to reach the great height at which their foes were flying. Allen had made this climb many times during the past two weeks, to engage in mock battle, but never so eagerly as now, when he flew to meet the thrilling reality. Up, up, straight into the sky he shot. He paid no attention to the three large bombing planes that were approaching him for his game was high up in the sky above him.

Leading his comrades by a hundred yards, he plunged into a group of ten German planes, opened on one with his machine gun, and passed through to attack a lone German airplane that was flying a great distance above the rest.

Up, still up, he climbed, straight at the German aviator, who suddenly dived at him. They trained their machine guns on each other simultaneously, and the shots glanced from Allen's engine as the German machine dipped beneath him. He turned, endeavoring to get his enemy in front of him, but the German skilfully maneuvered to keep Allen from opening fire. They flew around each other in circles, looking for an opening, and again the German raked Allen with his machine gun. Despite his slower airplane, he was more skilfull than the American.

Allen dived repeatedly, trying to come up on the German from beneath, but he only exposed himself to attack, so he circled again to keep the German from facing him. Suddenly he depressed his right wing-tip, and began to roll over. The German, seeing his adversary apparently collapsing, turned and poured a hail of bullets into the American plane. They did not take effect, but Allen's dangerous ruse brought his foe in front of him. As his plane righted, he shot upwards, like a hawk standing on its tail, and opened fire.

The German convulsively threw up his arms, for he was mortally hit. With a look of terrible agony on his face, he tore open his uniform and thrust his hand deep into his breast. He withdrew some small pasteboard object and pressed it passionately, to his lips. His plane fell earthwards, and Allen looped upwards just in time to avoid a collision.

The other enemy air scouts had been driven off, and the returning planes of Allen's comrades were visible in the east. Beneath him the darkness was beginning to flow over the landscape, pouring over every ridge and low-lying hill, streaming out from the highland and filling the chinks and hollows. The airdrome was dimly visible directly underneath him, in the pool of darkness that was rising steadily higher.

He began to descend, for his work was done. Unaided, he had won his first air fight and shot down his foe from the sky, while his companions had merely driven their enemies away.

As his biplane gracefully sped over the field and came to a stop, his captain threw aside military restraint and hailed him joyously.

"It is Freihofen," he shouted, "the best of the German aces, who has brought down more than sixty planes. You will be recommended for this, Lieutenant Allen, and the French will undoubtedly give you the Legion of Honor also, for most of Freihofen's victims were French. I want to thank you and give you my heartiest congratulations. Freihofen has been the terror of the French and English airmen."

Allen saluted, and strode silently over to the fallen airplane. The mechanicians were at work disentangling Freihofen's body. The machine had been smashed to bits by its drop of more than two miles, but the body showed few traces of its fearful fall.

The hands were still pressed tightly to the dead man's lips. Allen gently straightened the rigid fingers, one by one, and took from their grasp a small oval portrait. The fading twilight disclosed the laughing features of a beautiful German girl.

Allen received the congratulations and handclaps of his fellow officers in silence. He went at once to his quarters, a fire in his brain, and in his heart a fever. The girl of the portrait, to whom Freihofen's thoughts had flown in the moment of his death agony, might cry her eyes out, but Freihofen would never come back to her. How many tens of thousands of girls in the warring countries must wait in vain for their soldiers? Allen sat on his cot a long time, meditating. His face was wet with tears.

A COOKERY QUEEN

The Overland Monthly, December 1919

Time was when Standish MacNab was a tireless explorer among Chicago's eating houses. Memories of San Francisco drove him from one to another in search of something to remind him of the sea-girt city of the Golden West. For San Francisco is the best fed city on the continent, while Chicago, for its size, is the poorest fed.

On food, Standish spent careful thought and most of the income from his law practice. The greater part of what he ate he termed "grub." As for the rest, the service was slow, or the table cloths dirty, or the waiters surly; anyway, he found it hard to imagine himself in the Techau Tavern or Tait-Zinkand's. His gastronomic ramblings carried him into every cafe on Michigan boulevard, from the palatial Blackstone, where the waiters take themselves very seriously, to the Russian Tea Room and other pleasant sample establishments where one can enjoy the dainty portions served to him, if his appetite is not too big. In Marshall Field's tea room he sat among ladies who wore earrings and sealskin coats and stuck out their little fingers when they ate; he dined in cafes where heavy-jowled gourmands with bald heads and fat necks drank the juice from their oyster shells and gnawed the last speck of meat from their broiled lobsters; he also ate where hungry shop-girls counted out pennies for their meals, for his quest took him to the tops of skyscrapers and down into basement cafeterias. He nibbled at egg "fo young" in the Mandarin Inn and King Joy Lo's in search of something as tasty as the chop suey and bird's nest hoong chop blooey of Chinatown-by-the-Golden-Gate, but Chicago's almond-eyed waiters soon saw him no more. He manipulated spaghetti in Italian restaurants over saloons, and mourned the days before the earthquake (this word has disappeared from California lexicons) when for two-bits in the Fior d'Italia on the Barbary Coast he could eat a meal that shamed anything Chicago could offer for a dollar. He tried goulash in four or five Little Hungary restaurants, swallowed chicken and lamb a la Greek at Protopapa's, and wandered far from the "loop" to taste Venetian chicken at the Bismarck Garden. Time was when the young Chicago lawyer changed his eating-place thrice daily, but that was before he met Sadie.

Sadie was without doubt the most divine waitress that ever slung hash in a restaurant. She wasn't a raving beauty, yet despite that she had wonderful blue eyes like the sky seen from the top of Mt. McKinley; her smile was a stunner; her little pug nose was fascinating, and as for grace, she made all other waitresses look like Zeppelins and dreadnaughts cruising among the tables.

Standish stuffed a slice of bread into his ample mouth and stared in astonishment at finding such a sylph in a hashery. She was of that buxom type of women whose age cannot be judged from their looks. She might be twenty-three, or she might be over forty. Standish surmised that the lower limit was about correct.

His search for an eating-house was ended, and attacking forty-cent table d'hotes became henceforth his favorite pastime. The food was not better than otherwhere; in fact, an unprejudiced judge might have pronounced it a great deal worse. But Standish would not have rolled the College Inn, Kunz-Remmler's and the Boston Oyster House into one and taken the choicest viands from each in exchange for a daily seat in the Quality Lunchroom, after he first met Sadie waiting on the tables there.

"Whatcha going to eat?" she smacked.

"Just a minute—hm!—now let me see—nice restaurant you have here, huh?"

"Want our businessmen's lunch?" she questioned. "It costs forty cents, but it's real good."

She took his order, stuck her pencil into her hair—light brown, flavored with golden—and walked away, leaving Standish with his head in a whirl. He never had been in love before, at least not seriously, but this time the little winged boy had twanged an arrow with terrific force through his chest. Henceforth he thought and dreamed and lived tor Sadie.

Yet he dared not make love at once. She had not yet learned to reciprocate his affection, and besides, she might think he was flirting, and lose respect for him. So for the present he must be satisfied to leave a quarter for her on his plate, and get better acquainted later on.

Every day Standish ate in the Quality Lunchroom, except when urgent business called him elsewhere. He opened his thoughts to Sadie, told her his business, confided in her that he was making nearly $200 a month from his law practice, and would soon be able to get married.

But she never allowed him to talk of what lay uppermost in his thoughts. She would often sit opposite him and chat while he ate, after he had learned to come in during the slack hours, but she always found something to occupy her and take her away from him whenever he began talking about his heart.

Sometimes it seemed to him that the cashier, a man about the same age Standish, was narrowly eyeing his tête-à-têtes with Sadie, and he attributed it to jealousy. It worried him too, for he feared lest the young man, with his handsome face and gracile mustache, might already have the key to Sadie's heart. So he determined to bring matters to a head and declare his love.

Fifteen cents for breakfast and quarter each noon and evening. This was the unvarying amount of his daily tips. Sixty-five cents a day. Sadie did not lack spending money. Three dollars and ninety cents a week. She bought new hats, and sometimes forsook the movies for the Follies. Sixteen dollars a month. She could pay her entire confectionery bill with the lawyer's tips. Forty-eight dollars in three months. But here Sadie's pin money suddenly ceased, as it now becomes my heavy duty to relate.

At half-past three one afternoon Standish entered the lunchroom. Experience had taught him that the restaurant business was slackest at that hour. Luck seemed to be with him, for the other girls were out (gone to lunch, probably), and there was not another soul in the place besides Sadie and the good-looking, but jealous cashier.

Standish ordered eggs and coffee, and Sadie sat down opposite him to gather an earful of talk.

"Sadie," Standish began, "Sadie, what's the use of going on like this? You weren't meant to work in a restaurant. I want you to be my wife, and we can get a cozy flat up on the north side, and I'll buy a flivver, and—"

"Stop it," Sadie interrupted, rising. "Not another word about love. Not a word."

"But Sadie, don't you care for me?" Standish pleaded.

The cashier frowningly left his desk and strode toward

them.

"I like you well enough, Mr. MacNab, but I can't marry you. Because—"

She burst out laughing, and sank weakly into a chair.

"Frank," she gasped, when her mirth had somewhat subsided, "Mr. MacNab has asked me to marry him. Can you beat it?"

A sudden suspicion flashed into Standish's brain as he saw the angry face and threatening fists of the cashier.

"You aren't—already—married?" he gasped.

"You said it," she affirmed. "You can't blame me for laughing, Mr. MacNab, although I know it isn't a bit funny to you. I kind of thought you were in love with me, but—can't you see how funny it is?"

"I am deeply mortified," Standish confessed. "I apologize most humbly to you, and to your husband."

"My husband!" Sadie exclaimed.

"Yes. Isn't he your husband?"

The cashier shook with silent laughter, and Standish gravely surveyed him from the points of his patent leathers to the tips of his neatly curled mustache.

"My husband," said Sadie, "is the chef who owns the lunchroom. Frank is my youngest son."

Time was when Standish MacNab forgot San Francisco and her cafes de luxe, and was content to eat forty-cent dinners in a lunchroom under the elevated. But that time is also past, and a ceaseless hunger drives him from cafe to cafe, for the fire of hope burns bright in the breast of youth, and he still dreams that some day he may find a real San Francisco restaurant in Chicago.

IN THE DEPTHS

The Overland Monthly, December 1919

Dan Carlson looked down at the oily waters of Puget Sound and wondered what strange creatures lived in its slimy depths, and whether they were not really happier, after all, than he. A whirlwind racked his brain, for he faced involuntary separation from his job, and, being young, he was not used to it. For three days he had been a reporter on one of the city dailies—his first job, and he had failed on three assignments, so the city editor told him that he lacked aptitude and could not be used as a reporter. The boy pleaded for one more chance.

"I'll give you another chance," the city editor finally promised him, "if you go down to the waterfront and find a deep-sea diver named Angus McLeod and get his story of his fight with a devilfish three weeks ago. Look up the story in the files. Myers should have been able to interview him, for he has been marine reporter for years and ought to know everybody on the waterfront. But Myers hasn't been able to find him, and I can't tell you where you can locate him except that he ought to be somewhere on the waterfront. McLeod's story would have been a corker three weeks ago, but we can still use it."

Myers, the marine reporter, had learned only by chance of the diver's thrilling struggle with a giant octopus, and his rescue after he had lost consciousness, for McLeod was little known on the waterfront. The newspaper account of the battle under the waves was for the most part drawn by Myers from his imagination, for he had been unable to find and interview the dour Scot who was the hero of it.

Dan set out at once in search of McLeod, and he found that the old Scotch diver had moved from his lodgings several days before he was sent out on the job which so nearly cost him his life. Nobody seemed to know where he was living.

"He's about your height and pretty well tanned," the man in the salvage company's office described him to Dan. "He's got a grayish-reddish beard and he don't wear a mustache. He's an oldish fellow, a little bit deaf from being under the water so much, and he's got red hair and blue eyes."

On this meagre information Dan made the rounds of the waterfront saloons, but failed to find the man he was seeking. He did not want to go back to his city editor and report failure, so he stood on the wharf and speculated on the things that live under the water, and on his own drowning career.

The mystery of the ocean depths had always fired his imagination, but now it depressed him. He compared himself to the diver. The world was an enormous octopus, twisting its arms about his neck to drag him down. The breaking of the diver's air-tube was the fell stroke of chance, which had caused him to fail on his assignments and now prevented him from finding McLeod. Dan's star of hope, which had lit up his sky for an instant when he had been given this last chance to make good, was sinking fast behind vast clouds of gloom. Hardly a ray now lighted the muddy depths of his despondency.

Looking up from his gloomy musings he noticed a roughly-dressed, ragged man, unshaven, dirty and hatless, leaning against a pile. His torn shirt was open at the throat. A queer moaning gurgle came from his half-opened mouth.

He reeled as if he were drunk.

Dan feared the old fellow would fall into the bay, so he seized him quickly from behind, by the arms, just below the shoulders. The man shrank from his grasp with a moaning cry, and would have fallen from the dock had Dan not pulled him quickly back from the edge.

The stranger twisted around to face the youth, and he struck Dan's hands away as he did so. He gazed for an instant full into Dan's eyes with the fright of a hunted animal showing on his face. Then his gaze roved, and a puzzled, intent expression came over his face, as if he were vainly trying to recall something to his memory. He ran his fingers through his long, coarse hair and stared into Dan's eyes again. Dan noticed that the man's eyes were blue.

"You almost fell into the water," laughed Dan, reassuringly. "I guess you're sick, but at first I thought you were drunk when I saw you hanging to that post and reeling."

"Drunk?" asked the stranger. The intent, puzzled expression came over his face again and he rubbed his fingertips over his stubby, reddish-gray beard.

"Drunk?" he repeated, and his bewildered look became pitiful in its intensity and suffering.

"Oh, no! I mean I thought so at first—the way you staggered! Of course you're not drunk. But you did nearly fall into the water," Dan went on, hastening to change the subject. "You don't want to make fish-food of yourself, and be washed out into the sound where the devilfish can twist his snaky tentacles around your neck and little fishes come and swim through the holes in your skull, where your eyes are now."

"Fishes?" the man asked. "Oh, ay, there are millions of

'em, lad, millions of 'em! I've seen whole armies of 'em come and look at me while I worked, and one big fish came and looked in the little window to see what made the bubbles come up. But he swam away quick when I tried to grab him."

Dan was still deep in his gloom and took in the import of the old man's strange words only vaguely as in a dream. He looked up wonderingly.

"There are strange things down there in the depths," he said slowly.

"In the depths," moaned the old man. "Oh, ay, in the depths!" His eyes opened big and he stared at Dan as at some dreadful specter.

A flash of comprehension came to the youth as he pondered the stranger's peculiar utterance about the fish armies and the big fish that looked into the little window; and Dan suddenly noticed that the stranger's close-cut beard was reddish and that he did not possess a mustache. But his hair was not red—it was snow-white!

Dan's heart jumped and the star of hope suddenly flooded his firmament with light again. The clouds of gloom were dissipated as if by the fresh wind which was springing up from the sound. Dan's thoughts were no longer vague and wandering.

"Is your name Angus McLeod?" he asked his odd acquaintance.

"Ay," answered the diver, his eyes intently searching Dan's face.

"Carlson's my name—Dan Carlson," Dan introduced himself, his eyes sparkling. "Come over and have a glass of beer with me."

McLeod did not answer, neither did he clasp Dan's

outstretched hand.

"Come on," urged Dan, and he took the diver by the arm.

McLeod struck the boy's hand away as if in terror, but he followed him to the saloon. They were soon seated at a table and the bartender brought some beer.

"Now," demanded Dan eagerly, "tell me all about it."

"All about what?" asked McLeod.

"Why, about your fight with the devilfish up near Anacortes, of course."

"Oh, ay, the devilfish!"

The diver's eyes wandered; he looked terrified, and he passed his hands several times through his hair, then rubbed his stubby beard with his fingertips.

"Set 'em up again," called Dan to the bartender, for McLeod had drained his glass at a gulp.

"You were exploring an old wreck, weren't you?" he went on. "How long had the wreck been there?"

"Ay, a wreck it was. Several years old. It wasn't so awful deep, but I stayed too long."

McLeod ran his fingers through his hair again and horror was written in scarehead letters on his face.

"Come, come; you're all right now." Dan tried to calm him. "Drink your beer. Now go on. How deep was it?"

"Not too deep, for the sunlight was shimmering and shivering over the bones o' the ship, according as the waves was rippling and curling on top o' the water. It wasn't too deep, and there was a lot o' little fishes kept looking, and then they'd scamper away all of a sudden when they was frighted, like a lot o' minnows. But down in the ship it was dark and there was strange creatures there."

The diver shuddered and beads of sweat stood out on his

furrowed forehead.

"Drink some more beer," Dan urged.

The former intense bewilderment again furrowed McLeod's face as if something he was seeking kept hiding just beyond reach of his memory. He drank the beer and wiped the foam from his lips and chin on his sleeve.

"How did the octopus get hold of you? Tell me all about your fight with it. Nobody knows anything about it except what you told them through your diver's telephone while you were slicing the beast's arms off," Dan explained.

"Got hold on me? Oh, ay, it got hold on me all right," answered McLeod. "It must have got me from behind, because I didn't see it till it was around my neck. Long arms, like snakes, and it gets hold on me with two of 'em at once. First thing I knows about it, it draws me to one side, and I try to get away, but my feet are weighted and I can't move fast enough. But I'm just as cool as a clam. 'Never lose your head now or you'll never see Seattle again,' I says to myself. But it's hard to saw through those slippery, tough arms with my knife, though they look so soft and easy when the thing's captured and lying on shore, dead. But I've lost my knife," he moaned. "I tell you it's gone, and I can't pick it up."

The intent, bewildered look had again given place to horror.

"Come, come," Dan soothed him, "what ails you? Here, let me pour you some more beer. You say you had a knife?"

"I tell you I dropped it," exclaimed the diver with growing excitement. "Pick it up! Quick, I tell you!"

Pressing one knee against the table as if he were still struggling in the tight grip of the eight-armed monster, the diver gave a sudden push, upsetting the beer onto Dan, and sending his own chair backward onto the floor. He struggled to his feet with a frightened oath. As Dan sprang to help him, the diver seized his arms, pinning them to his sides and stared hard into his face, panting and shrieked—

"Where's that knife? I dropped it, tell you!"

Dan struggled to free himself, but the diver with wild, livid, staring eyeballs, held him fast. The sweat poured from the old man's face. Dan was thoroughly frightened and was about to call loudly for help when McLeod relaxed his hold and sank to the floor, moaning as if in agony.

Dan lifted him up and helped him to a chair. McLeod was as weak as a kitten. He stared helplessly around the room, while the sweat ran down his face in tiny rivulets. Boisterous laughter from the barroom explained why nobody had heard the struggle.

"Come, now," urged Dan. "You had a knife, you tell me, and you lost it. How did the air-hose break?"

"I cut it," McLeod answered, very slowly. "I didn't mean to, but the beast drew me towards him, and kept shooting a black, inky stuff at me, so by and by I couldn't see him for the dark clouds of it in the water. I sawed through three of its ugly hands, and I'll get away all right, only it's got me by the arm, and I've cut into the air-tube over my head, and I've dropped my knife and I can't pick it up.

"Where is that knife, lad?" he whined "There's no time to lose, for I've got no air, I tell you! They're pulling on the ropes up there, can't you feel 'em? Give me that knife! I've got to cut loose, I tell you! They're trying to pull me up, and the air-tube's cut, and I can't breathe, and I've got to cut away! Don't you hear me?"

He covered his face with his hands, moaning piteously.

"It's no use! It's no use!" he whimpered. "I've lost the

knife."

His unkempt, coarse white hair was wet with perspiration. Understanding began to dawn on Dan.

"Come, now," Dan said at last. "Nobody's going to hurt you. You're all right now. Tell me, how did you get to the surface?"

McLeod took his hands from his face and stared at Dan blankly.

"How did they get you up? How did you get to the top?" Dan repeated.

"Get to the top?" the diver moaned. "I didn't."

He covered his face again with his hands.

Dan felt a strange sinking of the stomach as he looked at the moaning creature before him, who was still fighting hopelessly on in his mind, with blank horror always at the end of his tale. For the diver's mind had given way under the strain of the desperate struggle under the waves and recorded no memories beyond that terrific combat, nor gave any glimmer of hope as to the outcome.

Dan had his story. And that same day tender hands took McLeod into their care and ministered to his overwrought nerves and anguished brain.

THE SILENT SHOT

The Overland Monthly, February 1920

"You say you heard no shot, Dr. Burns?" Wyatt asked.

"No," replied the young physician. "She must have held the revolver so close to her head that it muffled the sound."

"Strange," muttered the reporter. "Where was she when she shot herself?"

"Here in my office. I had just returned from some professional calls, and Helen got me some medicine to take up to my wife, who was ill in bed. The girl seemed despondent, but I didn't dream that she was planning to kill herself. I took the medicine upstairs, and neither my wife nor I heard the shot. I had not been gone ten minutes when the doorbell rang, and I came down to let in George Locke and his wife. The door into my waiting room was open, and we looked in as we went through the hall. Beyond, on the floor of my office, we saw poor Helen lying dead, and my pearl-handled revolver lay beside her. She had shot herself through the head."

"Helen Hume lived here in the house, then?" asked the reporter.

"Yes. She was an attendant in my office, and she stayed here. Her father and brothers live about four blocks down the street, but I don't think she got along very well with them. I think that's what made her despondent."

"How did she happen to have your revolver?"

"I suppose she took it to kill herself. Or maybe she wanted it for protection against burglars. I kept it under my pillow."

"How could Miss Hume take the revolver without being seen, if your wife was lying in the room sick in bed?"

"She could easily do that when she was making the beds. She helped around the house when there was nothing else to do. But you have all the information you need, haven't you?"

"Yes, I guess so. I have her father's address, and her age, and—oh, yes; where was the body taken?"

Dr. Burns gave him the address of the undertaker.

"May I speak to your wife?" asked the reporter.

"No, you can't go up there," Dr. Burns replied. "My wife is so terribly upset by the tragedy that she is on the verge of a nervous breakdown. She is so ill anyway that she was out of her head for a time, and this has given her a relapse."

"All right, Dr. Burns. Just one question more: do you think Miss Hume could have been shot by a burglar?"

"Oh, no, absolutely not," declared the physician emphatically. "She killed herself. I told you that she was despondent, didn't I?" he went on, growing slightly excited. "This is a plain case of suicide, and you won't get anywhere by trying to make a murder mystery out of it. Burglars wouldn't enter a house as early as 10 o'clock, anyway."

Ordinarily the reporter would not have gone to the undertaker's, especially so late at night. The case seemed to be an ordinary suicide, and he knew that at that hour, when the mail edition had already gone to press, a suicide story could get only a few lines unless it possessed very unusual features, or concerned a prominent person. But the girl's name sounded strangely familiar to him.

"Helen Hume, Helen Hume," he mused. "Why, that's the name of the little girl I used to play with in Cincinnati.

I think I'll run over and see. But it's probably only a coincidence in names, for I haven't heard that Helen was living in Chicago."

The undertaker was just going to bed, but he let Wyatt into his morgue when the reporter explained his errand. The girl was Helen, beyond any doubt, although she had changed much since he had last seen her. Now she was eighteen years old, comely, well formed, just blossoming into young womanhood.

Wyatt looked closely at her face. Suddenly his eyes opened wide.

"Look there!" he exclaimed, pointing to Helen's temple. "Did that girl kill herself?"

"You know as much about it as I do," the undertaker answered, and shrugged his shoulders. "I've seen many people that have shot themselves, but never one like this."

"So have I," said Wyatt. "Let me use your telephone."

"This is Wyatt talking," he told his city editor over the wire. "That girl didn't commit suicide. She was murdered."

"Who murdered her?" asked the city editor.

"I don't know. But listen—this girl didn't have any powder burns, and there isn't a hair singed, although the bullet went in at the temple, close to the hair. Did you ever see a person who had shot himself? Always terribly powder-burned, wasn't he? This girl must have held the revolver at least three feet away."

"That's good work, Wyatt," commented the city editor. "You may have a good story there. Keep after it, and see what else you can find. Ring me up if you get anything. Call back before half-past twelve, anyway, and turn in what you have."

Wyatt examined the body again. The bullet hole was as

clean as if it had been drilled with a gimlet. He recollected other suicides whose bodies he had examined. Always the bullet had spread and made a larger hole where it came out than where it went in. This shot, then, had been fired from across the room. It had taken a horizontal path, emerging at the same place on one side of the face where it had entered on the other side.

Wyatt held an imaginary revolver to his own temple, and found it hard to hold the weapon against his head with the barrel horizontal. While this fact in itself was not conclusive, yet, in connection with the clean, even bullet hole and the total absence of powder burns, it made Wyatt certain that Helen Hume had been murdered.

"Surely she was murdered," affirmed the undertaker. "I knew that as soon as I saw her."

Frank went over to see Helen's father, ostensibly to get Helen's photograph, but really to question him.

"So you're little Frankie Wyatt that used to play with my Helen, are you? I never would have known you," Hume greeted him. "Well, this is an awful shock to me. No sir, she hasn't been despondent, as far as I know. No, she didn't have any fellows, so it wasn't a love affair. I can't for the world imagine why she should want to kill herself. Surely she would have dropped some hint if she had been planning suicide. Oh no, sir, there was never any trouble between us. Was she murdered, did you say? Well now, sir, I'll say this much: she didn't have any reason to kill herself. If she was murdered, I want 'em to go to the bottom of it and find out who did it. No sir, I'm glad to hear you say that, because I'd hate to think poor little Helen had gone and killed herself."

Wyatt telephoned his story to one of the rewrite men on

the newspaper, quoting both the father and the undertaker as charging that the girl had been murdered. He cast no suspicions, contenting himself with trying to show that the girl could not have killed herself. His story was given a column, whereas the other two morning papers printed only a few lines about a "suicide."

Wyatt's account caused the coroner's inquest to be put over for ten days. The coroner was convinced that the girl was murdered; the undertaker was convinced; and the girl's father was convinced. But the police detectives assigned to investigate her death reported that she had killed herself.

Wyatt asked some of his friends on the detective force:

"Is it possible for a person committing suicide to hold the revolver so close to his head that there will be no powder burns?"

From one and all he got an emphatic no.

"It can't be done," they declared. "There is bound to be a recoil, and there will be ugly powder burns, no matter how close you press the muzzle."

"Can you muffle the noise by holding the revolver close?"

"Why, I suppose you can muffle it a little," assented one. "But see here, young fellow, if you're planning to kill yourself I can show you a way that won't hurt at all, and won't leave a sign to show what happened to you. You'd make a beautiful corpse."

"Thanks," said Wyatt. "I don't care to shuffle off just yet."

"Helen Hume wasn't killed in a love quarrel," he told his city editor, "for she had no sweethearts. The theory that she was shot by burglars is silly. I don't think Dr. Burns killed her, but there are some peculiar things about this case that make me suspicious. One is that neither the doctor nor his wife heard the shot, although he admits that the door was

open into the office when he passed by with Mr. and Mrs.
Locke. And then his preventing me from seeing Mrs. Burns
set me wondering. Maybe she is really sick, but her husband
gives me the impression that he just doesn't want anybody
to question her."

The coroner's jury, when it finally sat on the case, refused
to turn in a verdict of suicide, despite the police report. The
jury found that Helen Hume came to her death "as the
result of a shot from a revolver, fired by person or persons
unknown," and recommended that the police investigate
further to find out who fired the fatal shot.

Wyatt's convictions concerned the murder and not the
murderer. As to who the slayer was he harbored only vague
suspicions, which he could satisfy only by examining the
physician's house. This the physician forbade. So Wyatt put
the girl's death out of his mind as one of the unexplained
murder mysteries which often crop up to puzzle reporters.

"Do you think you can find out who killed that Hume girl,
if I let you work on that alone for two or three days?"
demanded the city editor, several days after the coroner's
jury turned in its verdict.

"I might. I'd like to try," Wyatt answered.

He boarded a street car and went at once to Helen's
father.

"Mr. Hume," he said, "I want to ask you frankly, have you
any suspicions as to who murdered Helen?"

"I think Dr. Burns did it," Hume replied. "I don't know
who else could have done it. Somebody did it."

"What kind of a woman is Dr. Burns' wife?"

"Why, she seems to be a nice little woman. But you
surely don't suspect her? I might think her husband did it,

but not Mrs. Burns."

A few minutes later, Wyatt tiptoed softly up the doctor's front steps and tried the door, but found it locked. He could see a light in the parlor, and a newspaper, behind which he surmised Dr. Burns was sitting. Then the telephone bell rang, and Dr. Burns got up to answer it.

Wyatt silently withdrew into the shadow. The doctor came out, carrying his case in his hand. Wyatt slunk around to the rear door. This was unlocked, and he entered the house without knocking.

There was a back stairway leading down to the doctor's office, as Wyatt had supposed. He turned the doorknob and entered, closing the door behind him. Then he opened the door from the office into the waiting room, and the door from there into the vestibule. The front stairway was in plain view from the office.

Did some strange acoustic vacuum intervene between him and the front stairs, so that a shot fired in the office could not be heard upstairs? This question was almost immediately answered for him by the voice of the doctor's wife calling from upstairs. Lightly though he had moved, yet she had heard him.

"Robert," she called down. "I thought you had gone out."

A minute of silence ensued.

"Robert," she called again. "I wish you would come up to me."

He returned no answer. Presently he heard her coming up the back stairs. He slunk behind the office door.

"Robert," she called again. "Where are you?"

She entered the office and switched on the lights. She gave a little shriek when she saw Wyatt, and she stood in the middle of the floor in her nightgown, opening and closing her mouth, as if she wanted to speak. Her face was white, and Wyatt observed also that she was thin, that her eyes bore a haunted, scared look, that her face was drawn and careworn, although she was still a young woman.

"Who are you, and what do you want?" she finally found voice to ask.

Wyatt closed the door.

"I want to know why you killed Helen Hume."

Mrs. Burns put her hands to her head as if in pain, and stood for more than a minute silently rocking back and forth on her heels. Then her strength left her, and she would have fallen if Wyatt had not caught her. He helped her to a chair, and brought a glass of cold water, which he held to her lips.

"Who are you? And why do you come here to torture me?" she exclaimed indignantly, pushing away the glass.

"Don't excite yourself, Mrs. Burns. I see that it really was true that you were too ill to testify at the coroner's inquest. I had thought it was merely a bluff to keep you away."

"Who are you?" Mrs. Burns asked again.

"My name is Wyatt. I am an old friend of Helen Hume. Why did you kill her?"

"What right have you to enter my house this way, without warrant and without invitation?"

"In cases of this kind, Mrs. Burns, one does not wait for invitation—Helen Hume was standing over here when you shot, wasn't she? And then you fled up the back stairs while your husband faced the police, while he shielded you and kept you from being interviewed, and invented a suicide story that can't hold water. Why did you kill Helen Hume?"

"Mr. Wyatt, leave my house this instant. Such affrontry is unpardonable. The girl killed herself."

"Did you see her do it?"

"No. I was just going upstairs when I heard the shot."

"You *heard* the shot?"

"No, no, no! I don't mean that. There wasn't any shot. I didn't *hear* the shot, I mean."

"Then you were *not* upstairs sick in bed. You were down here."

"I wasn't down here, I tell you! I was going up the stairway when she shot herself."

"That is enough, Mrs. Burns. Your husband said that you were both upstairs, and that you were in bed. But you tell me that you were on the back staircase. Your husband says that neither of you heard the shot. You tell me that you heard the shot, and then, remembering that your husband's story was different, you deny that you heard it. You say that you were there on the stairs and knew when it happened, but your husband pretended that he discovered the body when he came through the hall with Mr. and Mrs. Locke. As a matter of fact, your husband left the corpse of the girl to answer the door bell. He led his visitors through the hall, and then, when they saw the body lying in a pool of blood in his office, he pretended that he was seeing it for the first time.

"Mrs. Burns, I am a reporter. If I print the statements you have just made, flatly contradicting your husband, he will be arrested. The police will naturally suppose that he was the girl's murderer. Otherwise why should he lie and pretend that he had not heard the shot, and knew nothing about her death?"

"You say my husband would be suspected?" the doctor's wife asked, her eyes big with fear.

"He will be convicted. He is already suspected, because

of his fishy story about not hearing the shot when all doors were open between him and the office where Helen was killed. The fact that he perjured himself will execute him. Many men have been sent to the chair on less evidence."

"You won't do it! You shan't do it! You mustn't drag my husband into this! I swear to you that he had absolutely nothing to do with the shooting! His murder will lie on your soul if you bring this unjust suspicion on him!"

"I am only after facts, Mrs. Burns. If your husband is innocent, why does he conceal the facts? It is because he is protecting you. You were jealous of Helen Hume. You thought your husband was too fond of her, and so you shot her. Isn't that so? You will do him a still greater wrong by keeping silent now. I can't vouch for his fate if you still refuse to tell me why you killed Helen Hume."

"I didn't shoot her deliberately! I didn't, I swear I didn't! I am not a murderess! I was out of my head, but even so I didn't intend to kill her. I was arguing with her, and trying to scare her with the revolver. I didn't even know it was loaded. Don't, please don't print anything, Mr. Wyatt! It was purely an accident! Enough unhappiness has been caused already, without adding this."

Wyatt heard a noise, and, turning, he saw Dr. Burns standing in the doorway.

"You're in mighty fine business!" the young physician exclaimed, shaking with wrath. "Mighty fine business, breaking into a house to make a sick woman confess to something that isn't true! What are you going to do?"

"That depends on you and your wife," answered the reporter. "I want to know all the details."

"There are no details," replied the physician. "My wife and I were happy, until this tragedy happened. My wife has been very ill. She was not responsible for the shooting, for she was delirious when it occurred. You can't get a conviction on the evidence you have, but the publication of a story such as you want to print would ruin our lives. There was an unnatural situation here—a beautiful girl, just developing into womanhood, living on terms of intimacy with a young married couple. The intimacy was nothing more than a strong friendship, but at that it was an unnatural situation to have her living in the same house. My wife's illness made her supersensitive, supersuspicious. And she was out of her head when poor Helen was shot.

"There is nothing more to tell. But consider this—the coroner's inquest is over, and unless you revive the matter the police will make no further investigation, and it will soon be forgotten except by us. You hold our happiness in your hands."

"What success did you have?" the city editor demanded when Wyatt showed up in the local room next day. "Did you find the murderer?"

"I have talked with the doctor's wife," Wyatt answered. "She was my last clue, and I have followed it out as far as I can. Please give me another assignment."

MOTHER

The Light, March–April 1920

Josephine found her position as a chorus girl in McLoskey's Theater a welcome change from waiting on fussy women in the millinery department of Marshall and Company. Not only did she receive eighteen dollars a week, which was just eight dollars more than the department store paid her, but for the first time in her eighteen years of life there was variety and spice to existence. Her associates and environment were a pleasing relief from the drab monotone of her home life.

There were no enjoyments in her home. The motto, "God Bless Our Home," set in an ornate gilt frame, watched over the living room. The walls were covered with garish wallpaper, and bedecked with cheap chromos. A pink tissue paper shade, renewed at intervals, drooped over the table lamp, and a horse-hair couch sprawled across one end of the room. The house was always scrupulously clean and neat, for Josephine's mother took great pride in her little home. The two lived comfortably and quietly on Josephine's wages and the small pension which the kindly, white-haired widow received from the government. They owned their little house, and the mother, wrapped up in her daughter, gave genuine love and affection.

But distractions were lacking, and her home life was gall and wormwood to Josephine. The taste of wine was unknown there, and her only dissipation, before she left Marshall and Company, was an occasional movie with her mother. Josephine was wearied of this humdrum existence, tho she would not for a great deal have complained to her mother; so she got into McLoskey's theater thru a girl friend who had been taken on there.

Now she was tasting life. Existence was in every way more enjoyable. She did not stand on her feet for nine hours a day, and she did not have to smile at customers who wrought on her nerves until she wanted to scream.

She gloried in her emancipation from the slavery of the department store, and quickly became used to wearing tights. Her whole relation to the world had undergone a change. Young men now saw her to her home at night after the show, a thing which never occurred when she worked in the store. She danced with them in cabarets, and drank—a liberty she was not allowed at home, and which she never mentioned to her mother.

Her mother was usually asleep before Josephine got home. Only one night did she wait up for her, and Josephine did not get home before 2 o'clock. Her mother did not like the appearance of the boy that escorted her, with whom she had been dancing and drinking. She was outspoken in her criticism of him, at breakfast next morning, and made fun of his pasty complexion, his pale, characterless face, the nonchalant stoop to his shoulders, the hair slicked back smoothly over the top of his head, and the cigaret that hung from the corner of his mouth. Josephine said nothing, but she could not help thinking her mother unjust. This type of fellow gave her a good time, which she never had from the twelve-dollar-a-week clerks at Marshall and Company's.

The stage-door Johnnies came around during rehearsals, and chatted and flirted with the girls. She loathed them at first, but, with increasing familiarity with her tights and greater confidence in herself, she was soon at ease with the stage hangers-on. It no longer perturbed her when strange men stood in the wings and stared at her legs, but rather she came to take pride in their comeliness.

One of her girl associates in the chorus told her that she was a little fool, when she declined an invitation to dinner at a cabaret. But that was when she was new in the chorus. She soon became familiar with the bright lights and the taste of cocktails and rich food. She even accustomed herself to the lewd stories told by both girls and boys, which shocked her at first with their filthy suggestiveness.

Sometimes involuntary shudders went thru her as she looked at the hard faces of some of the older girls, and she was resolved, come what might, that she would never tread the path of easy pleasure which they had trod. They had gone down, and down. As they became more and more unbeautiful they painted the more in a vain effort to keep the appearance of beauty. But already they found it hard to attract men to spend money on them, while the younger girls, like herself, were much sought after.

One day, when a group gathered about the piano, before rehearsal, Josephine picked out from a pile of music a coarse song, and sang it. With gestures, wriggling of body, facial grimaces and rolling of eyes, she brought out the full suggestiveness of the song, making it inexpressibly filthy and lewd. Her companions roared with laughter, and applauded vociferously. She had to sing it again. She outdid her previous effort, and her audience of chorus girls and hangers-on crashed and shook with mirth. Some of the girls were even shocked.

The stage director stood watching her, as she repeated the song, and he applauded more heartily even than the others.

"Say, kid, that's hot stuff," he commended her. "I'm going to feature you in that song. Why, if you come out on the stage in an evening dress and sing with all the motions you made just now, they'll go nutty! It's you for a solo act when we change the bill next week."

Josephine was on the heights. She had been in the chorus just a few weeks, and already she was to be featured in a solo part. Success and fame were beckoning to her, and she had visions of herself as a bright star in the Broadway firmament. The other girls crowded around her to congratulate her, and she knew that in their hearts they envied her.

She could hardly wait to tell the good news to her mother. The white-haired widow was immensely pleased at Josephine's good fortune. She plied her daughter with questions. When was she to sing the song? Would it mean a raise in wages? Did it imply a future advancement? It seemed she could not learn enough, so eager was she, and she repeated her questions over and over, her eyes shining with contentment and joy.

A rehearsal of the song seemed fully to satisfy the stage director, who predicted that it would make an instant hit.

Monday night came, and Josephine went perfunctorily thru her steps in the chorus, for her mind was on her song.

"I wonder who is that white-haired old woman in the front row?" one of the girls commented, when they came off the stage. "I don't see what *she* sees in this kind of a show."

McLoskey's Theater was indeed not the kind of show-place to attract white-haired old women, for its reputation was far from savory. A vague dread gripped Josephine, who had been so excited in anticipation of her own stunt that she had not noticed the spectators at all. She was to go onto the stage with the chorus once more before her solo turn came, and she would have a good look at the old woman.

It was her mother! There she sat, looking at nothing, thinking of nothing, but her daughter. Josephine could see that she was smiling encouragement to her. The girl suddenly became conscious of her skirtless tights, conscious that she was exposing her legs before a theater full of men.

She scarce knew what she did, as she tripped thru the steps with the other girls of the chorus. Then she retired to change into an evening gown for her special act.

She could not sing that vile song, and make those filthy and suggestive motions, before her mother! The depths to which she had sunk were revealed to her, and she saw before her an abyss into which she was about to tumble headlong. All was clear to her now. She had already trod far in the path of degradation. The cabarets, the bright lights, the wines, the coarse dances, the vile companions, the lewd stories, the low men with whom she associated—all pointed to but one end. A chasm was yawning for her, or was she not already falling into it, beyond any chance of saving herself? No, for was she not still a virtuous girl? Might she not hope some day to marry, and leave this life? She saw all too clearly the wretched future that would await her should she marry a man of the type she met in the cabarets and at the stage door. How low she had fallen already! She was about to proclaim publicly her lack of moral sense by singing a song so vile that she would rather die than sing it before her mother!

Tearfully, in an agony of apprehension, she clawed over a pile of trashy songs. Somebody shouted to her. It was time to go on the stage. She picked from the pile a song that she knew. She would sing that, for she could not sing the filthy song expected of her. Clasping the sheet of music to her heart, she half walked, half staggered, onto the stage. Her brain was spinning as if she had been drinking poor wine. In a daze she went to the piano, and agitatedly handed the music to the pianist.

"I'm singing this instead of the other," she said in a harsh stage whisper.

The pianist glanced at the song and looked up at her half incredulously. She was already before the footlights waiting for him to begin.

Her eyes were brimming with tears, and she sang straight to the heart of the white-haired woman sitting in the front row, whose only thought was of her daughter.

The melody was cheap and trashy, the words were mawkishly sentimental, and the girl's voice was throaty and raucous, but the song went to the heart of her for whom it was intended.

The audience was not impressed. A woman laughed. Men yawned and looked bored. The song was out of place in that theater. Tawdry and worthless as music or poetry, still it played on the old theme of the love between mother and child. Those who came to McLoskey's Theater did not like to be reminded of the theme.

> "'M' is for the million things she gave me;
> 'O' means only that she's growing old."

The stage director was glowering in the wings, biting his finger nails.

> "'T' is for the tears were shed to save me;

'H' is for her heart of purest gold."

The business manager had gained the stage door. He burst on the stage director like a hurricane.

"'E' is for her eyes, with lovelight shining;
'R' means right, and right she'll always be."

Still that throaty voice quavered on, and the tears brimmed up in the eyes of a white-haired woman in the front row, who sat utterly oblivious of the painted faces around her. The rest of the audience were suffering from boredom.

"Put them all together, they spell 'Mother',
A word that means the world to me."

The vials of the business manager's wrath were emptied on the stage director's head. The discussion rose until the voices of the two could be heard in the front rows. Josephine's mother was too intent on the song, however, to hear them. She was wiping her eyes, and endeavoring in vain to hold back the tears. Josephine began the second stanza.

"It ain't my fault, I tell you! The poor fool grabs up the music an' rushes onto the stage with it, after I'd trained her up careful in that 'Shimmy, Jimmy' song. It ain't my fault, nohow!"

"Well you could have prevented it," stormed the manager. "Thank God, she'll be thru in another minute," he added irreverently.

"'E' means everything she's done to help me;

'R' means real and regular, you see;
Put them all together, they spell 'Mother,'
A word that means the world to me."

A little perfunctory applause followed her as she left the stage. She ran into a thunderstorm in the shape of the irate manager and stage director.

"Hey, Tetrazzini," said the manager, with withering sarcasm, "you've got a rotten sense of humor, if you think you can sing."

"You're fired!" shrieked the stage director, so angry that he could scarcely speak. "You're fired, y'understand? You, you —————!"

He spat out a filthy name, which smote her like a whiplash, and capped it with a vile oath.

Josephine stifled a cry. To think she could be called such a name! Never, not even in the low stories she heard from her stage associates, had so filthy a word been uttered. She blanched with anger and mortification, and clenched her hands until the nails bit into her palms. But the invectives had just begun, for, as she stood there white with humiliation and shame, her breast heaving, her heart full of bitterness and pain, the manager and stage director in their anger called her every filthy name they could think of.

She finally burst into a storm of tears, and groped her way to the dressing room, which she shared with several other girls of the chorus. She sobbed violently, and wished the other girls gone. She could not tell them why she had not sung the vile thing expected of her. She did not want their condolences; she wanted only to be let alone.

She got into her street clothes, and powdered her face to hide the tear stains, but fresh tears continually welled from her eyes and rolled down her cheeks. How could she face the lights of the street-car in such a condition?

There were no hangers-on at the stage door as she went out, and for that she was thankful. The few passengers on the street-car looked at her curiously as she drenched her handkerchief with tears, and strove to repress her sobs. One man came over to her, and tried to comfort her, but she repulsed him, and went out into the night. She walked the rest of the way to her home, and humbly thanked Providence that the night was dark and hid her distress.

Her mother was home before her, for she had not waited, after Josephine's song was sung. That, and that only, was what she had gone to the theater to hear.

She was filled with exalted happiness, for her daughter was a success. Josephine had sung a song that touched her heart, and made her cry, and the woman's simple soul did not understand that others had not been so moved.

Josephine put her head on her mother's breast, and sobbed out the whole sordid tale—the cabarets, the drinking, the lewd stories, the filthy song she had been supposed to sing, and the unutterable humiliation put on her by the manager and stage director. The white-haired widow took the girl in her arms, and the gap, which had been insensibly widening between them, was closed. Heart to heart they talked, and Josephine held nothing back from her mother.

"Ah, Josephine," said the woman, "if you had only kept me in your confidence, day by day! But are you sorry, dear, that I lost you your place, by going there to hear you sing?"

Josephine smiled thru her tears. She looked around at the chromos on the wall, at the pink tissue paper lamp shade, the horse-hair sofa, the ornately framed motto. Then she turned back to her mother. Poor and unpretentious it was, but it was home, her home, where she was steeped in love and affection. Impulsively she threw her arms about her mother's neck, and hugged her.

"Oh, mummy!" she exclaimed. "You saved me from myself. Tomorrow I'm going back to the department store."

Her face shone with happiness. Her mother held her in her arms, and crooned an old lullaby, as she used to do years before. Her child had come back to her bosom.

OUT OF THE FRYING PAN

An Operatic Tragedy

The Overland Monthly, May 1920

Fortunio Duo was an operatic tenor. That does not explain how he happened to be owing a thousand dollars to his hotel, for he received that much every night he sang, according to the newspapers, and he therefore ought to have found it easy to pay his bills. But the tenor was all but broke, and the hotel was guarding his trunks until he should pay up.

He was promised two thousand dollars for a two weeks' engagement as guest artist in a neighboring city, where he was to make his first appearance in opera the next day. This was twice as much money as was needed to pay his bill at the hotel. But the hotel managers, who were pigs without appreciation of art, would not release his trunks. So Signor Duo, he of the musical name, laid his head to his pillow and wept. He wailed aloud in his anguish of soul, and called down curses on the pigs who treated him so shamefully.

How came the tenor to be penniless when he received one thousand dollars a night? He had sung fifteen times during the operatic season just ended, and simple arithmetic shows that he should have been paid fifteen thousand dollars.

Unfortunately, the rules of arithmetic did not apply. The newspapers simply were misinformed about Signor Duo's salary, for they had accepted the statements of the opera company's publicity man at their face value. Signor Duo's contract called for fifteen performances, but three of these were to be sung gratis, and for the other twelve he was to be paid two hundred and fifty dollars each, or one-fourth what the newspapers declared he received. Out of this he had to pay his manager ten per cent.

And he gave Mr. Doppler fifty dollars a week to furnish paid applauders. Of course he did not *need* a claque! It was an insult to suggest that he, the great Italian tenor, could not get applause without buying it! But—suppose the claquers should hiss him if he refused to pay? That was different, and Signor Duo was very grateful to Mr. Doppler, who knew the ways of these Americans, for saving his singing from being ruined by a wicked and unprincipled claque. He also gave Mr. Doppler fifty dollars a week to bribe the newspaper critics into saying pleasant things about him. In his simple soul he supposed there would be not the slightest difficulty in buying favorable notices. But Mr. Doppler knew better, and put the money into the Doppler bank account, and the newspapers saw not a cent of it all.

Mr. Doppler was secretary and assistant to Signor Parmese Pescatore, the great Italian maestro and operatic director. The maestro was of course too exalted a personage to stoop to graft, but—he hired Mr. Doppler as his secretary.

Of the three thousand dollars allowed to Signor Duo in his contract, the tenor received in actual cash only seventeen hundred dollars. He had to advertize in several musical journals, as all important singers do. He had to buy many high-priced costumes. He had been mulcted by a fellow patriot who wanted funds to back a benefit for Italian war orphans, and ran away with his collections. But why enumerate all the ways in which a tenor spends money? Suffice it to say that he still owed the money due to the musical papers that carried his advertising, that he owed money to his tailor, his hotel, his music teacher, and everybody else who had dealings with him. The only people that had collected from him were his manager and Mr. Doppler. The manager was paid only through the courtesy of Mr. Doppler, who deducted the manager's commission from Signor Duo's salary and sent it to this gentleman after he (Doppler) had first taken one-fourth of it as a collection fee. Alas that there are so many Dopplers in this vale of tears!

One might well ask why the tenor did not leave his trunks and his troubles, board the train, sing his two weeks as guest tenor, and then get his baggage back by paying his hotel bill. The reason he could not do so is because his costumes were in those trunks, and without costumes an operatic tenor is of no more use than a drum major in overalls.

Many schemes went through his perplexed brain, but one after another he had to abandon them all. He wiped his perspiring forehead on a richly perfumed handkerchief, sprayed perfumery on his clothes, sat down on his bed, and wept.

Then a dread assailed him—what if this superfluity of sobs were affecting his voice? So he opened his mouth and began to shake forth Canio's lament from "I Pagliacci," the opera in which he was billed to open the next night. He stopped, dismally, as the import of the words was borne in on him: "Tu sei pagliaccio!" (You are a clown!)

"No, pagliaccio non son!" he sang, and resumed his interrupted flow of tears. There came a knock at his door, and he hastily powdered his face to conceal the stains of weeping, sprayed perfume on his hair, and quavered, "Come in."

It was his friend, Carter, a newspaper reporter who sometimes breezed around the opera house in search of stories and features about the "nuts," as he called them. He blew into the tenor's room at this dismal minute like a breath of fresh air.

"Ah, Meester Carter," exclaimed the tenor, in his inimitable French-Italian accent; "I am in trooble, Meester Carter, mooch trooble, and I wish you should help-a me. Ah, you will aid me! Now I can be happy once more, for I have leaved it to you! You will find-a ze way! Tra-la-la!"

"What's up?" Carter queried.

"Ah, Meester Carter, I must to sing in 'Pagliacci' tomorrow night. But I cannot to take ze trunks from zis hotel. And all my costumes, zay are in ze trunks, and I must not leave ze city wizzout ze costumes. I owe it to ziss hotel mooch money, and zay hold ze trunks until zay have ze money. But now I leave it all to you, and you will make it arrange. Oh tra-la-la," he sang merrily.

Carter thought the tenor was giving him a pretty stiff assignment, but he tackled it with spirit.

"You be here in your room tonight at 10 o'clock, without fail, and I'll fix it for you," he promised after a minute of reflection, which was punctuated by the tenor's warblings.

Carter reserved a room, as he went out, for Miss Cecily Jones of Milwaukee, and about 10 that evening he came into the hotel with a young woman of the operatic chorus, who registered under the name he had chosen for her. She ordered her trunk and two suit-cases taken up to her room. Carter smuggled the key to the tenor. Then he accompanied the young woman to the nearest elevated station, and escorted her to her home.

Signor Duo worked hard that night. Packing trunks and suit-cases is a tedious job for a tenor who has no valet to assist him. In the morning he came down to the hotel desk.

"I eat here no more where nobody not trust me," he snapped to the hotel clerk. "I go eat-a my breakfast outside in ze restaurant. Some time, I make you mooch trooble—mooch trooble!"

In the morning Carter's friend of the chorus also made her appearance at the hotel, and paid her bill—out of the little money yet remaining to the tenor. She ordered her trunk and suit-cases sent to the railroad station, and Signor Duo took charge of them there. A happy smile lighted his face.

"Ah, zoze hotel peegs!" he exploded. "Now zay will wait wan long time for ze money! You will see."

The tenor's soul was at peace. He sat in the parlor car and enjoyed the beauties of the landscape. Joy had returned to his world. And he would get his revenge on those grasping hotelkeepers, for they would wait, wait, wait, a m-ee-leon year, before they got any money from him.

Signor Duo arrived in good time at his destination. He sent his trunk to the theater and his suit-cases to the hotel, and notified the opera company by telephone of his arrival. Then he went to his hotel and washed for dinner.

Never had life seemed so rosy. He was about to conquer a new city, to bring new hundreds of music lovers under the potent spell of his voice. He pictured to himself the many curtain calls he would receive, the salvos of applause, the cries of "bravo," the adoration of the women, the handclaps of the orchestra. He glanced at the pictures of himself as

Canio and Don Jose, in the evening newspapers, and read the exaggerated reports, prepared by the press agent of the local opera company, which seemed to him truthfully accurate, of his successes in New York and other cities. He ate his dinner with more than usual relish, tipped the waiter bountifully, and set out on foot for the theater where he was to sing, stopping several times to admire the announcements on the billboards heralding him as "Italy's Golden-voiced Tenor." It was indeed a happy day for Signor Fortunio Duo.

As he neared the theater, the crowds increased.

"They come early to the opera here," thought the proud tenor. "The press agent his work well done."

He quickened his pace. There were more people in the streets, and still more, hundreds of them, thousands, and all hurrying in the same direction.

"Where stands the opera house?" he asked an excited urchin who came rushing by him round the corner.

"Just around the corner," shouted the boy, "before it took fire. The front wall is just fell in."

Signor Duo staggered under the blow and almost fell between the wheels of a fire-engine rushing up to answer a general alarm.

He wiped his damp brow with his perfumed handkerchief and reflected that it was indeed a most merciful dispensation of a kind Providence which made him a waiter before he took to the grand opera stage.

THE STOLEN MELODY

The Overland Monthly, November 1920

It is hard to believe that there ever was a time when Mascal was not a musician. Yet the world of music was an undiscovered country to him until after his twentieth birthday. He used to run the night elevator in the Occidental, an old-style apartment house in a part of the city formerly wealthy, and still retaining much of its gentility, though fallen on evil days. Somber gables stared a mute protest at the upstart modern flats which stood at the end of the block; the walls were chastely papered in a plain, dark pattern; and an elevator jerked hesitatingly from floor to floor under the uncertain propulsion of an iron rope.

Hard though it is to believe that Mascal at one time in his life knew nothing about music, it is still more incredible that he lacked ambition. Such, however, is the fact. In the drowsy atmosphere of pride and decay which hung heavily on the apartment house, Mascal had seemingly no higher aspiration than to remain an elevator boy all his life. The guileless expression of face, which still characterizes him, seemed to contradict the nobility of his finely sculptured head; his gentle blue eyes contrasted strangely with his brick-red hair; and from these soft eyes gleamed at times the dreaming soul of a poet. Why Mascal, of all men, should bury his light in so trivial an occupation as running an elevator is beyond comprehension. How many unearthly sweet melodies must have been lost to the world by his utter lack of desire or ability to set them down on paper!

Mascal did not play any instrument. He could not sing,

for his voice was unmusical. Written music was like Chinese hieroglyphics to him, and he had never heard an opera or a symphony orchestra. The music of the vaudeville theaters sounded tawdry and coarse to his sensitive ear, but he liked some of the old tunes, such as "Swanee River," and "Old Black Joe," and he used to whistle Dvorak's "Humoresque" and an aria from "Il Trovatore" until they became banal. He learned few new tunes, and most of these were torture to him.

Mascal was better pleased with the tunes that welled up out of his own brain—soulful melodies, which sang themselves to him, possessed him, and grew and developed as he whistled them. They came to him on walks in the suburbs, amid the roar of street traffic, or when he was alone in his elevator at night. Then they passed out of his mind, except *the* melody.

This particular melody was no better than many others that had come to Mascal, but he could not banish it from his thoughts. It haunted both his waking and sleeping hours, wove itself into his dreams, and molded his musings. Metz, the violin student who lived in the same boarding house, wanted to know the name of the tune he was whistling, and Mascal did not know what to tell him. Mascal took the melody, at the advice of Metz, to a musician who made his living by transcribing music, supplying parts for orchestras, arranging and harmonizing. He charged Mascal only five dollars, and for this he not only wrote out the melody on manuscript paper, as Mascal whistled it to him, but he also supplied a piano accompaniment for it.

Mascal was now, in a sense, a composer. Metz played the melody on his violin, and showed him what the notes meant on the keyboard of the boarding house piano. Mascal was fascinated at finding meaning in each little tail to the notes, and logic in every dot and line. The hieroglyphics were taking on significance.

He took enormous pains in mastering the characters on that sheet of music. He easily learned to play the melody with his forefinger; but the chords in the accompaniment, the synchronizing of his fingers, were so difficult that they almost disheartened him. His fingers refused to strike the right notes.

When he had learned to play the piece, in a manner of speaking, very slowly, with frequent pauses to rearrange his fingers on the keys, it annoyed and depressed him. He began to experiment with different chords, and found that he could better the transcriber's arrangement. But he did not know how to set down the harmonies that were in his mind, so he left it in its unsatisfactory shape, and whistled other tunes as he went up and down in the elevator—snatches of airs from the operas, as he had heard them in cafe orchestras, and old-time tunes; but mostly he whistled phrases that gushed unbidden from the depths of his own consciousness.

It was in a vaudeville theater that he heard his tune again. At first he thought it must be only a coincidence, in the opening measures; but no, it was his melody which the girl was singing in her throaty, disagreeable voice. All the beauty had gone from it. It was twisted and tortured out of its original form, set to disgusting verses, and the girl was ragging it, debasing it, shouting it at the audience, dancing to it and making eyes as she sang, to bring out the risqué suggestiveness of the verses. The audience clapped and stamped and yelled for more, and the creature sang additional verses.

The tune was catchy, cheap and trashy! His brain was hot with anger. As he went out of the theater with the throng, people were humming his melody. If it had only been sung in its original form, and set to noble verses! He was ashamed of it now, and enraged by the debasement of a theme that once had haunted him by its sheer beauty.

Mascal sought out Mueller, the man to whom he had paid five dollars for transcribing his melody, and protested vigorously. He was met with insolence. Mueller defied him to prove the melody his.

"Mr. Mueller," Mascal explained, a menacing glint steeling his gentle blue eyes, "it is not that I object to your making money out of my melody. But you have robbed it of its beauty. You have set it to filthy words. My melody was majestic, singing, beautiful. You have made it a cheap thing, a nothing.

Mascal's accusation brought Mueller to his feet.

"You upstart!" he bellowed, the fat folds of his bullneck purpling, and his little pig eyes narrowing in the red ocean of his puffy face. "You, what do know about music, hey? You can't play—you can't read—you have to come to me to write your tune on paper. Now you try to tell me what to do with it, hey? I made it popular. Less than one month it is printed, and one hundred thousand copies are sold. Hey? In three more months I sell a million. Get out of here, you, you—"

Mueller was shaking a pudgy forefinger under Mascal's nose, and Mascal's anger flamed hot within him. His clenched fist caught the melody-thief under the chin, and knocked his across a chain. Mueller bellowed for help, and Mascal hastily retreated down the stairs.

Perhaps it needed just such a burst of anger to break the

chains that bound the slumbering genius of this easy-going boy. Certain it is that ambition came to him then for the first time in his life. It was no selfish resolve that he made that day, for it brought him pain and suffering, sleepless nights and days of hunger. He would devote his life to vindicating his melody before the world. The tawdry thing was even now a torment in his ears, as whistled by the driver of a passing taxicab.

Mascal smiles reminiscently when he thinks of the months that followed. But he did little smiling then, for he spent the greater part of that disheartening time in shiny clothes, underfed, often wondering how he was going to get his next meal. But it is a glorious thing to be possessed by a dream.

Most of his little bank account went to pay his tuition at the musical college. He had to learn from the beginning. They let him take up piano and violin playing, but they told him it must be a year before he could begin the study of harmony, for he had no preparation for it. He never became a great player. He seldom touches his violin today, and he still finds his fingers stiff on the piano. But he studied hard, and read harmony and musical history on the side, and they let him begin harmony lessons within four months.

He soon discovered that he could read harmonies away from the piano. They sang themselves to his eye. He nearly fainted from excitement the first time that he ever read a measure of chords away from the piano and pictured the harmony in his mind. He rushed to the piano to verify the harmonies that his eye had sung into his brain. He began to be able to play all of his pieces in any key, for the notes that were written on the staff sang into his ear before he struck the ivory and ebony keys of the keyboard.

He possessed, far more valuable than familiarity with the classics, the ability to evolve melodies out of himself. Each new musical discovery thrilled him, and he never lost his enthusiasm, despite his privations. He applied himself so diligently to harmony and composition that he left the class behind him, and had to take private lessons. These cost more money. His bank balance was used up, and the money he earned as night elevator boy was not enough to keep him properly and pay for his lessons also.

He moved into an attic room for which he paid one dollar a week, and another dollar each week went for the privilege of practicing two hours a day on a piano. He began going without his breakfasts, and occasionally he had to skip his evening meal. He became woefully thin, and darned his cheap cotton socks with coarse thread when the holes got large, for he could not afford to throw them away. The Chinese laundry tore his shirts and saw-edged his collars. He did his own cleaning and pressing, and his clothes became smooth and shiny. He carefully polished his shoes each morning, but more than once he went to his lessons with his shoe laces knotted in three or four places, to postpone the expense of buying new ones.

His privations depressed him, because he could not see the end. But when he was studying he forgot everything except the beauty that was burning in his soul.

He earned his teacher's praise for the intrinsic beauty of the original themes on which he elaborated, even when the elaboration was unskillfully done. His pet delight was to disguise the stolen melody and elaborate it, but always his teacher rebuked him, saying that the theme, which he recognized as the tune of a distressingly vulgar popular ragtime air, offended his ear whenever and wherever he heard it. Each such rebuke inspired in Mascal a gnawing dread lest his sacrifice and struggles be in vain. He lost hours of sleep trying to make noble arrangements of his melody, but the teacher's eye sought them out under each disguise, and always branded them as tawdry.

Mascal had been studying a year before he ever heard a symphony. He plucked up courage to ask for his teacher's ticket for a day when he knew the teacher would be absent from the city. He did not realize what important results his request would bring, what further sacrifices and what marvelous joys were to be his.

He watched the different themes enter and leave as the orchestra played an overture, but it was simply greater playing than he had heard in the orchestra of the musical college. It was followed by Beethoven's Fifth Symphony. Mascal heard the striking of the first four notes. They were repeated, in a lower pitch. Then the strings took them up, playing them quickly, in ascending series, and the first movement of the symphony finally came to an end without varying from the one little theme of four notes. Can four notes make a whole composition? he asked himself. But as he listened he realized that they were indeed the soul of the movement, now sung by the strings, now sounded by the brasses, now shouted in chorus by all the choirs at once. Little themes sprang from them, and the orchestra returned to them. The movement was a composite whole, as different as may be from those sugary impromptus that begin nowhere, end nowhere, and have no excuse for being. The world of harmony that followed the opening of these was predestined in the first four notes.

Mascal realized that this symphony would lose its glory if played on the piano. The color of the different instruments gave it life, soul, feeling and beauty. If a great master can develop a whole movement of a wonderful symphony from four notes, like a knocking at the door, why could not he do equally wonderful things with the wail of the wind, the roar of the waves, and the murmur of leaves in the trees?

He obtained a miniature score of the symphony from the library of the musical college before he went to his room that afternoon, and studied the staves that represented the different instruments. Now they played in unison, now in harmony; now each choir was divided off from the others; now one choir played a counterpoint against the others. He did not know the instruments well enough to hear in his mind their tone colors, but already he had decided that his melody, when it stood vindicated before the world, would not be written for piano. He would make of it a tone poem for orchestra.

Underfed though he was, yet he skipped two evening meals during the next week, and with the fifty cents thus saved he bought a seat up near the roof to hear the next symphony concert. The happiness that came to him that day with the realization of his own genius never left him from that time.

The symphony was Schubert's Unfinished, the great song-writer's orchestral masterpiece, discovered years after his death. Instead of hearing a plain theme majestically developed, Mascal's ears drank melodic beauty from the first movement. The symphony sang straight into the beauty-loving soul of him, and tears rolled unabashed down his cheeks, for the great idea had come to him.

Beautiful melodies were uttered by the strings, and sung by the orchestra with a piercing sweetness of tone such as he had never dreamed. This man, this Schubert, must have gone to the angels in heaven for his themes, for the outpouring of beautiful sound as far surpassed in sheer beauty anything within the narrow limits of his knowledge as the odor of wild roses on a country roadside surpass the smells of a city street. Every stroke of the violins, every chord of the music that sent the salt tears trickling down his cheeks, sang to him:

"You are another such master! No music, be it harmonized and developed to the uttermost limits of the theme, can move the unfeeling world unless it be founded on melody. To you the world looks for the supreme musical outpouring, for melody comes to you as easily as song to the throat of the meadowlark. You are the melodic master of the world."

Mascal knew that it was true. All his life he had been thrilled by the beauty of his own themes. His mother, in those pleasant days before he was orphaned, used to smile happily when he came into the house whistling some strange and lovely rhythm, and remark, "Ah, my boy, why do you not learn to play the flute? How pretty that would be on the flute!"

He did not hear the rest of the program. He threw himself on his bed and dreamed, until it was time for him to work. He dreamed while he was running the elevator; he dreamed in the early morning while he was undressing for bed; and when he fell asleep his melody was shouted to him by a bevy of flutes. He awoke to hear a passing teamster whistling it in its dance-hall garb.

Mascal no longer built on the stolen melody for his work at school, for he knew that his teacher, having heard it in its street dress, would brand it as trivial no matter in what gorgeous apparel it were presented to him. But he starved himself further to take in the symphony concerts each week. He lived for them, and for his melody.

He studied the scores in the music room of the public library, and tried to pick out the different instruments as they sang the themes. He found that reading orchestral scores was a different matter from reading piano music. The themes jumped disconcertingly from the horns at one end of the page to the strings at the other, and other instruments came in between with notes that only careful study revealed as mere accompaniment or harmonic background. He had to learn a third clef. He found it hard to read the chords, for the notes were distributed among different instruments, on different staves. But by diligently comparing the scores with the actual playing of the orchestra he began to find order in the chaos. Best of all, he began to recognize the tone-colors of the different instruments, to learn what was uttered to the ear by different combinations of instruments, and to divine the function of each of the tone scheme.

Even before he learned this he was working on his symphony. He tried to orchestrate his melody the same week he heard Schubert's symphony, and he failed because he did not know the meaning of the different instruments. A piccolo to him was a small flute, and he could not differentiate between the parts owing to the oboe, and those that should be given to the clarinets. Yet he worked on until he had completed a first movement to his symphony. The foundation of it was the melody that had been hammered out in every dance hall from Florida to Alaska.

It must not be supposed that Mascal's First Symphony at that time was more than remotely similar to the great work which the world now knows as the Melodic Symphony. The same melody dominated the first movement, but the melodic theme was the only likeness between the two. However, the completion of this movement gave him a sense of triumph, and in the joy of it his mind sang with melodies that welled up joyously like a gurgling fountain. He wrote four more movements within as many weeks, and every page of the score was permeated by beautiful themes. One will look in vain through Mascal's First Symphony for the amazing counterpoint that distinguishes his later works, but it still remains the favorite of all his compositions, for even Mascal has written no more melodically wonderful symphony than this, which is a way of saying that it is the most melodious composition in orchestral literature.

But the writing of a symphony could not be accomplished by one so inexperienced. Mascal had to work at it through many months, and he discarded practically all of the scoring that had cost him so much effort, leaving only the bare melodies that sang so sweetly in his dreams. That wonderful variation in the first movement, where the pilfered melody is shouted full-voiced by the entire choir of woodwinds, with a counter melody picked out on the strings, was not added until the very week before his interview with Koruloff.

The first meeting between Mascal and Koruloff should be marked as the happiest date in music since Wagner decided to build operas on the German myth-lore. One year and a half before that meeting Mascal could not read the notes on the staff, and neither he nor Koruloff had heard of each other. On the one hand a boy, not yet twenty-two years old, holding out with faltering hands the score of his symphony, and stammering a frightened explanation of why he had dared to take up the time of the conductor; on the other hand the bluff old musician, who for fifteen years had guided one of the world's greatest symphony orchestras.

Mascal turned the pages and showed the master where the theme changed from one group of instruments to another, and hummed each new theme and variation. The master smiled as the boy turned page after page, but he said nothing until Mascal came to the end of the first movement.

"You have never studied the instruments of the orchestra, I perceive," he commented, a peculiar smile playing on his face.

Mascal gulped. Was his work in vain?

"I—I am learning to play the violin," he stammered, "and I—I have come often to the concerts, and I have followed the instruments with the scores."

"The general effect is good," smiled the master reassuringly. "But you have given to the trumpets and horns notes that they cannot play. This passage runs too low for them, and you repeat your mistake on the next page. If the brasses tried to play this passage here, of a sudden you would have stopped notes, exactly as if they had caught cold. And here, in this passage for the bassoons—what effect are you trying to get?"

"Wh—why, the bassoon adds richness and beauty to the passage," he explained.

"Then put the passage down. The bassoon can serve your purpose very well, but not in this range. It can give depth and richness to the tone picture, but it is a fickle instrument, and its upper tones are ghastly. If your symphony pictured a gloomy castle, with bats flying around the haunted windows, and you wanted an uncanny and ghostly effect, you could get it from the upper notes of the bassoon. Put this phrase down into the lower part of the bassoon's range, and you will obtain the rich effect you want."

Mascal was reassured, and Koruloff began to examine the other movements. The wealth of melody in them was beyond the range of his experience, although he knew by heart and could conduct without his scores more symphonies than any other conductor in the world. So prolific in singing melodies had been the brain of the young composer that he had not taken the trouble to develop many of them, but had written them as simple themes or introductions to other themes, and passed on to new side themes in his recapitulation of the leading melodies.

Koruloff gave him much advice as to the scoring, showed him why different instrumentation in parts of the work would bring out its beauties better, and even pruned away several choice melodies, which are now among the best of Mascal's songs. He suggested changes in the treatment of certain of the themes. But the fabric itself, the framing, the melodic and harmonic structure, and even the scoring, were fundamentally sound, and Koruloff promised to produce the symphony in the autumn. He was so impressed that he postponed his vacation several days to help Mascal, and within two weeks the work was scored. Koruloff took the manuscript with him that summer.

The symphony was not presented until late in the winter, and what happened at its presentation is common knowledge. The number of times Mascal was called out to acknowledge the demonstration can be equaled only in the annals of grand opera, when a Patti or a Galli-Curci is forced to show herself twenty times in front of the curtain after repeating some unusually lovely aria.

How the critics hailed the work as the supreme triumph of orchestral music, how the composer leaped at one bound to be the recognized leader of the musical world, how this super-Beethoven brought American music into its own—all these things are well known. But what the world has never known is why Mascal chose a tawdry ragtime melody as the theme of his sympathy. Some critics have seen in it an attempt to prove that no melody is tawdry, and they use specious reasoning to show that Mascal took the most trivial tune he could find and developed it into one of the majestic themes of music. Others argue, with equal heat, that Mascal built on a popular theme to prove that the music of the people is really the only great music after all. But what none of them has understood—and that is why this account is written—is that the melody was never tawdry. It was a noble melody from the first, and Mascal simply restored it to its primal estate.

THE MEDAL OF VIRTUE

Munsey's Magazine, December 1920

I

"A package for Mlle. Josephine Duprez!"

The three men and three women who were making merry in the café raised their eyes questioningly. A champagne cork popped.

"A package for me?"

"For you, certainly, if you are Mlle. Josephine Duprez," said the postman, shaking the rain from his cape.

The girl lifted her glass for a quick sip of champagne, and rose. Her gown was cut low in the front and back, and the train dragged.

"A birthday present! A birthday present for Josephine!" shouted Yvette, letting herself fall sidewise into the arms of her male companion.

Every one laughed uproariously, as if Yvette had said something immensely clever. It was evident that the liquor was already going to their heads, although it was only mid afternoon, and Josephine's birthday party was to last far into the night.

"Is it from you, Amédée?" inquired Josephine. "How original you are, to send it to me through the mail!"

She leaned over to plant a kiss on his cheek, but her aim was bad, and the kiss fell on his open mouth. Every one laughed again. Amédée threw his arms around her, and squeezed her until she cried out. Struggling from his embrace, she ran to the postman, and snatched the package from his hand.

"*Merci, monsieur le facteur*," she thanked him. "But, *parbleu*, this looks more like a letter than a package! Are you sure it is for me?"

"It is for you, certainly. Ah, thank you, *monsieur*," he added, as Amédée poured him a glass of champagne.

He shrugged his shoulders once again to shake off the rain, and touched glasses around the table.

"To your very good health," he said; "and to the felicity of *mademoiselle*, for I perceive it is her birthday party."

"I am twenty-one," said Josephine.

The postman drank his champagne in little sips, smacking his lips, and chewing the bottom of his mustache, not to lose a drop of the sweet liquor. He drained the glass; then, bowing low, he went out into the blustering storm that was drenching the city of Orléans.

"Open the package, Josephine."

"Open it. A ring, I'll wager!"

"From the Emperor of China!"

"No, from the President of France!"

"From the hunchback in the Rue St. Germain—the one that makes moon-eyes at her!"

A peal of laughter greeted each of these sallies. Josephine succeeded in undoing the package. It contained a little bronze medal. The accompanying parchment proclaimed that the Society of Jeanne d'Arc for the Encouragement of Morality had bestowed on Mlle. Josephine Duprez the medal of virtue in recognition of her many good deeds.

"A medal of virtue for Josephine!"

Her companions shrieked hilariously, and fat Albert's voice went out in little flickering gasps at the top of the scale.

Yvette tore the medal and parchment from Josephine's hands. Her comrades all tried to read at once.

"For the encouragement of morality!" barked Amédée.

"Our Josephine has become a saint!" Yvette proclaimed.

"Hail to our little St. Josephine!" cried Jacqueline with mock reverence.

"For virtue!" piped Albert, between gasps.

Josephine stood bewildered. A crimson flush became visible under the rouge on her cheeks.

"A medal of virtue for Josephine!" gurgled Paul, convulsed, as if he never had heard of anything so ridiculous.

"She is blushing! She is blushing!" screamed Jacqueline, clapping her hands.

A hot surge of anger flamed up in Josephine. She snatched the medal from Albert's fat fingers.

"No matter what I am, I am not what *you* think!" she exclaimed.

Clasping the medal to her breast, she ran out into the street.

II

A cold spray smote Josephine's forehead, but it was a full minute before she comprehended that it was raining. She stopped to rest, breathing hard, for she had been running. A rude wind drove the rain into her face, and a storm of resentment made turbulent riot in her heart. A tousled dog barked at her, and a sudden quickening of the shower sent the cold rain trickling down her neck.

Who was *she*, to be awarded a medal of virtue? How well justified her companions were in laughing! A cocotte, a card cheat, a liar, a thief, she believed her withered soul incapable of noble thoughts or noble deeds. The medal was certainly not for her. She must restore it to its owner.

She hurried through the streets, oblivious of the rain that

was beating upon her and pouring down her back in little rivulets. She knew, though her companions did not, that there had once been another Josephine Duprez in that quarter. To her the medal belonged, for her good deeds were known throughout the city, although few knew her by her real name. She now lived in the big convent two miles away, near the Loire, where she was called Sister Dolores. It was to this convent that Josephine turned her steps.

A pair of gendarmes looked curiously at her as she hurried through the rain in her low-cut evening gown, spattered with mud, her train dragging over the wet cobblestones, her long plume sagging heavily before her chin. She was thankful that the rain kept the people out of the streets. Her heart gave a little jump of exultation as she realized that in returning the medal she was doing at least one virtuous deed.

She caught occasional glimpses of the great Gothic cathedral which looms over Orléans. Its massive spires seemed like fairy tracery, even from near at hand.

As she hurried furtively across the corner of a public square, her eyes fell upon an equestrian statue of Jeanne d'Arc, the patron saint of the city, whose life and death are portrayed in the cathedral's stained-glass windows. The cheerful light of a Jeanne d'Arc bakery winked at her through the falling rain. She passed Jeanne d'Arc hotels, Jeanne d'Arc bookshops, Jeanne d'Arc cafés. The whole city seemed to do homage to the white soul of the maid, "La Pucelle d'Orléans," whom Josephine, in a low jest, had named "*la plus sale d'Orléans.*" She muttered a swift prayer to the saint whose memory she had dishonored, but checked herself with a pang of fright. Would that spotless maid receive a prayer from one so fallen?

She reached the convent in a state of agitation bordering on hysteria. She hesitated a minute on the steps. Then, summoning courage, she rang violently. A nun appeared.

"Sister Dolores!" exclaimed Josephine. "I must see Sister Dolores!"

Sister Dolores was out in the city, ministering to the poor, Josephine was told; but she insisted.

"I must see her!" she cried, almost fiercely, clutching the medal tightly to her breast. "I have come all this way in the rain to seek Sister Dolores. Where is she? When will she return?"

The nun, judging from the girl's agitation that the matter was urgent, gave her three street addresses, and Josephine set out again on her search.

She passed through a squalid quarter, choosing the narrower and less frequented streets. The rain was driving down with increased violence, and Josephine's wet clothes clung to her flesh. A panic fear assailed her lest she might not be able to find the good nun to whom the medal really belonged. A gnawing sense of depression followed the exhilaration caused by the champagne.

She found herself at last in a lane so narrow that she could touch the houses on both sides by merely extending her two arms. The walls seemed to press in on her, and a great weight lay on her heart.

She knocked at the first of the addresses, and inquired whether a sister of charity had been there. A child, half-clad and ill-fed, motioned up a dark stairway. Josephine crept up to the landing, and knocked at the door. Her heart was beating wildly. The door opened, and she found herself face to face with Sister Dolores.

III

Josephine staggered weakly toward the sweet-faced nun, but for a minute she could not utter a word. Then she held out the medal in both hands. The parchment was crumpled and dripping.

"For you!" she cried. "The medal!"

Sister Dolores looked at her curiously. The plume of her hat sagged heavily across her face, dripping water. Her gaudy gown was water-soaked and mud-bespattered. Her train was soiled and tangled. Her bodice, cut low, showed the heaving of her breast as she held out the medal to the nun.

"For you! The medal of virtue!"

Sister Dolores seemed not to understand.

"Sit down, my poor girl," she said. "Then you can tell me what it is all about."

Josephine did not take the proffered chair. Two or three starved-looking children huddled in a corner, frightened at this sudden apparition. Josephine stood in the center of the room.

"They made fun of it—of your medal! The postman brought it—for Mlle. Josephine Duprez; but it is not for me—it is a medal of virtue. I—I knew your name was Josephine Duprez—like mine—and it must be for you. They all made fun of it—Amédée and Albert and Paul, Yvette and Jacqueline—so I took it away from them."

Beseechingly she held out the medal and the damp, crumpled certificate. The water dripping from her garments formed a pool on the floor.

"It was my birthday party," she continued. "I went to the convent, and they—they said you were here—and I came—

to find you—to give you the medal."

The nun gazed at her in pity, seeming puzzled.

"Don't you see it must be for you?" Josephine implored. "Look!"

She opened the water-soaked parchment.

"'Mlle. Josephine Duprez,'" she read. "'For her many good deeds.' Ah, that is for you! And the postman—he brought it to me—at my birthday party. I—I am a—a—but you would not understand! I am the worst! Yes, it has come to that! I steal at cards. I look over the men's shoulders when they play. I signal to Amédée what cards they hold. For five years I have led this life. And I was bad before that. I steal—I lie—I sell myself. And the postman brought me a medal of virtue! But I knew it was for you."

The nun took the parchment, still uncomprehending. She smoothed it out and read it. Josephine turned to go.

"Wait, my sister; you must sit down and rest," said Sister Dolores. "You are tired and wet. You have come a long way in the rain."

"Yes, a long way," repeated Josephine absently.

She remained standing.

"You have made a mistake," said Sister Dolores tenderly, after a pause. "This medal is for you."

"No, no, no! It is for virtue! See, where it is engraved: 'The Medal of Virtue!' It is given for good deeds!"

"Are you then incapable of good deeds?"

"Assuredly, for, look you, I am a—a bad woman. I live in sin—it is my occupation. I am lost beyond hope. Pray for me, sister!" she exclaimed, sinking to her knees in a sudden access of terror. "Pray for me! I am lost! I am lost!"

"And yet—you left your birthday party to bring me this medal—in the rain—clothed as you are?"

"It was yours, Sister Dolores. I could not keep it."

"Are you not Mlle. Josephine Duprez?"

"Yes, but the medal was for virtue! That could not be for me."

"You could have kept the medal. You could have had

much mirth over it. You could have ridiculed it with your companions, and added to the gaiety of your birthday party."

"But it was not for me, sister! Itbe longed to you."

Sister Dolores held out her arms.

"My poor child! You deceive yourself," she said. "You say there is no good in you, yet you left your birthday party to restore this medal to me. You have spoiled your happiness and angered your friends; you have walked miles in the rain; you have made yourself miserable to do a simple deed of duty that you could easily have left undone. Yet you call yourself lost to noble impulses. Do you not see the springs of good in your nature? In truth, the medal belongs to you. You have earned it."

She forced the medal into Josephine's hands. The girl's pent-up feelings broke their gates, and swept away the reserve she had frantically tried to maintain. She flung her arms about the nun, sobbing violently. Her breast heaved; her heart was pounding. She poured her sorrow and remorse into the sympathetic ears of Sister Dolores. Her years of shame stood out like sickly specters before her awakened eyes, and she saw her wasted life in all its black ugliness.

But when the storm of tears had spent itself, and the passion of grief had moderated, her face was alight with new hope. The nun's words had uncovered hidden waters, and Josephine realized that she was not incurably evil. She still had good aspirations; she still was capable of noble thoughts and actions. With that realization came the knowledge that her old life was gone like a tale that is told.

Arm in arm with Sister Dolores, she left the house, and these two daughters of Eve passed out into the storm together.

THE POLE-STAR

The Open Road, February 1921

We all have heard the story of the surgeons who killed a condemned felon by suggestion. They pretended to open a vein in his arm, and made him think he was bleeding to death. Physicians say the story is not true, but whether it actually took place is beside the question. It is an example of the power of suggestion, and since the summer when John Whittern and Arvid Williams and I were camping together I have realized from my own experience something of the power there is in suggestion.

John was a handsome fellow, six feet tall, athletic, well built, with clear, healthy complexion, big, frank blue eyes, and very light yellow hair. A sculptor would have joyed to watch the play of his muscles underneath the white skin. He was whole-souled and generous, light-hearted and care-free, always bubbling over with good humor, and everybody liked him.

We occupied an old cabin on a lake in the north woods that summer. I guess perhaps we got a little tired of hunting and swimming and sleeping, for we walked ten miles into town to drink pink lemonade and watch the elephants at the circus. In one of the side shows we found a withered old fortune-teller, who pretended to read the past, present and future for half a dollar. Her face was puckered like a dried apple, and about the same color; her thin hair was a dirty gray; her wrinkled hands, with their long nails, were an offense to the eyes. The things she told John were worded so vaguely that they might mean anything or nothing. John thought he was not getting his money's worth, and he poked fun at her predictions. She looked up at him darkly, her eyes narrowing to thin slits, through which the pupils showed dull black. Extending her skinny hands before her, she exclaimed tragically:

"When you next see the pole-star, you will die!"

You may well believe that John was amused. He thought that prediction was the funniest thing he had ever heard. The first thing he did that evening, as we started back to

camp was to look for the pole-star, but it hid behind a cloud.

"Star-dust," he explained jocularly, "is the most ancient poison in the universe. Its power was known when the pyramids were mere brick-babies. It killed the Cæsars, and put the quietus on the Roman Empire, according to the astrologers, and I hope it poisons the composer of 'Bedelia.' That old crone at the circus, if she knew how to direct the influence by which she claims to read the future, might commit stellar murder on whomsoever she wished; and she could rule the world if she had brains to boot."

John talked on like this until we begged him to stop. Meanwhile the clouds spread and grew heavier, and John was forced to postpone his astrological suicide.

For several days it drizzled, and no stars were to be seen. Then the weather gradually cleared, but meanwhile the fortune-teller's prediction had slipped out of our minds.

The lake on which we were camping resembled roughly a capital L, one arm of which pointed south, the other, east. Our cabin stood at the corner, or elbow, toward the northwest. Directly across the water, about half a mile distant, was the wooded point round which the lake bent. It was the inner edge of the elbow-joint, as it were, where the shore bit deepest into the lake. A seldom-used trail wandered eastward from our cabin, circled the upper bay, and passed within a quarter of a mile of the promontory. Between the trail and the water, however, there was a thick growth of brush and brambles, through which even a goat could hardly fight its way.

One hot evening, about a week later, Arvid and John had

gone swimming. I had caught a fish-hook in my foot that morning, imbedding it so deeply that it had to be cut out. If you ever had a similar experience, you will know that I didn't feel like swimming. I sat out on a camp-stool in my bathing suit and tried to keep cool and fan the mosquitoes away, while the other two went for their swim. I envied them, out under the twinkling stars, where the mosquitoes could not follow, or the heat oppress.

A light breeze came dancing over the water, and cooled my forehead. Someone dragged the canoe into the lake. I could not see which one had taken it, for the moon had not yet risen, but I heard the swift dip of the paddle for a few seconds as it sped toward the opposite shore.

I heard Arvid hallooing. His voice became fainter and fainter in the distance, and I wondered why he was calling. Suddenly I noticed the pole-star shining brightly, and I recalled the fortune-teller's prophecy that when John saw it again he would die. I pondered for what seemed a long time, until I half feared that the prophecy might mean more than we had supposed, and that John might actually be in danger.

The breeze stiffened to a light wind, and I became chilled, for I had been sitting on the camp-stool a long time with the cool air blowing on my body. I limped painfully down to the shore, where the water was lapping in melodious ripples on the gravel.

Soon I heard Arvid returning. He grounded his canoe, and stepped out beside me, looking like a white ghost in the darkness. His teeth chattered, and he did not see me until I called to him as he was starting for the cabin.

"John's dead," he said.

"Dead!" I ejaculated. "What are you talking about?

How . . ."

"It was the pole-star."

Arvid shivered

"How did it happen?" I cried, disregarding his allusion to the silly divination of the fortune-teller. "John is too good a swimmer to drown on a calm night like this!"

"I know he is; but I've been out in the canoe for nearly an hour, hallooing all over the lake, and he does not answer."

"There's a chance that he was taken with cramps and landed somewhere on the other shore," I suggested.

"There's no chance, for he would have answered my hallooing if he were on shore. He is dead, and it's that dried-up hag at the circus who made him die."

It angered me to hear Arvid at this tragic moment carry on about the fortune-teller's absurd prediction.

"This is no time for nonsense, Arvid," I growled. "How did you come to lose him? You were together when you started out."

"We struck across toward the point."

Arvid threw out his arm toward the dense thickets on the opposite shore.

"I was swimming easily, enjoying the coolness, and John was splashing ahead and had gone far beyond me. I was about half way across when I first noticed the north star, but John must have been nearly to the point. I tell you I was startled, for in a flash, as I looked at the star, I remembered what the old woman at the circus had said. I thought I heard John call out, and I hallooed back, but he didn't answer me. I swam back here as quickly as I could, and got the canoe. I have been all over this end of both bays; but John is lying somewhere on the bottom.

"I know what happened, just as well as if I had experienced it myself. You remember how amused John was when the old woman told him he would die when he next saw the north star? Well, John didn't see the north star that night, or the next night, for the sky was heaped with clouds. And it slipped out of his thoughts, just as it slipped out of mine until I saw it tonight.

"Now I'll tell you what happened. John turned on his back to rest. Then he saw the pointing stars of the dipper, just as I did, and his eyes followed along them lazily until they rested on the pole-star. Then he remembered what the old woman had said.

"You know John well enough to know that it takes more than that to frighten him. He wasn't frightened—yet. He just laughed. And then he turned over on his face and swam again. But when he looked for the light in our cabin, it wasn't there. You forgot to light it. He must have wondered which way the cabin lay, for there was no moon to light us."

Arvid stopped speaking and slapped his arms vigorously across his chest; he was shaking so from cold that his words sounded chill and shivery. I was too agitated to reply. Then Arvid continued, pushing each syllable out through his teeth.

"Not seeing the light must have confused him; and whenever he turned on his back to rest, he saw the north star, and it kept him thinking of the prophecy. Don't you see what happened then? He noticed that he was getting tired, for he had been swimming hard, and the water is mighty cold tonight after you've been in it a while. Just hear my teeth chattering. Well, he began to shiver, and he started back toward the cabin. But the cold, and his weariness, and his failure to see the light in our cabin, began to make him wonder, just a little bit, whether there might be something in the fortune-teller's augury. And he began to swim a little harder, and got tired more often, and every time he tried to rest he saw the pole-star again.

"Don't you see that it could end only one way? He must have been nearly half a mile from here when he first saw the star, and he tried to fight his way back with a powerful stroke that would tire even the strongest swimmer. When this breeze came up, and the water began washing over his face, he became completely scared, and lost his head. He died, not because he saw the polar star, but because he had been *told* that he would die when he saw it."

Arvid's recital had become almost incoherent, so hard was he shivering. The breeze had come up strongly now, and I, too, was cold, for I was clad only in my bathing suit. We went into the cabin, I hobbling, and Arvid still shaking from cold.

"Good heavens, man!" I exclaimed when he had lighted the lamp. "You are as white as a sheet."

We talked in low tones until nearly midnight. We recalled the thousand and one little kindnesses that one loves to remember in a departed friend. We decided that Arvid should take the news to John's father, leaving me in the cabin for a few days; and I was secretly glad that my foot was cut, so that I should not have to carry the tragic message.

The moon rose, and every tree cast its long shadow along the ground. We heard something shuffling slowly along the shore, and Arvid went to the door with his rifle, thinking the prowler was a bear. Instead of a bear, the tall figure of a man came slowly toward us from the trail that skirted the shore of the upper bay. We were startled at having a visitor at this dead time of night, in our out-of-the-way camp, but when the figure came into the lamp-light we saw that it was John.

"I'm back again, fellows," he called, and staggered into the cabin.

His face was smeared with blood from an ugly gash over his left eye. He was bleeding also from several smaller cuts. His bare arms and legs were badly scratched, and his chest was torn by briars.

We were immeasurably relieved to see him, you may well believe, but his ghastly appearance alarmed us. We helped him to his bunk, and he sank down on it with a sigh of relief.

"It was the north star," he replied to our anxious queries. "Warm up some water to wash out this gash in my forehead, and I'll explain what occurred. Do you remember that fortune-teller's prediction about what would happen to me when I saw the pole-star again?"

Arvid and I exchanged glances.

"I had swum nearly to the point before I noticed the star. I hadn't given it a thought since the night when we came back from the circus. It winked at me as if to say, 'Well old fellow, here I am, and you can't get away from me.'

"Boys, I frankly admit I felt a strange sinking of the stomach when I saw that little point of light trembling at me across the bay. I realized all of a sudden how far away from camp I was. I looked toward the cabin, but I couldn't see the light. I trod water, and turned round and round. I can't describe the eerie feeling that possessed me. Turning round in the cold water, in the black night, with nothing in sight but the stars, I lost my sense of direction, and called out for Arvid. There before me shone the north star, like a judge pronouncing sentence, and I was alone and cold and tired in the lake, perhaps half a mile from camp. The thought flashed on me that the fortune-teller had told the truth, and I was really doomed. I cried out for help. Then a black bulk loomed out of the darkness and I swam to it and pulled myself out upon the point over yonder.

"Boys, I would have stayed on that point all night rather than try to swim back. The north star would have been in front of me all the way to camp, if I had swum, and it fascinated me so much that I could not have kept from looking at it. It seemed to dare me to come into the water. I suppose I was foolish not to call for help; but after all I knew that my feeling about the star was nothing but a silly superstition. I wouldn't for worlds have gone back into the water, and yet I was determined that no one should know what a fool I was making of myself. So I turned my back on the lake and fought my way through the bushes to the trail.

"A person would be a fool to try to break through those bushes even in broad daylight, with thick top-boots and khaki pants and coat; but I did it in the dark, stripped naked with not even a bathing suit to keep off the thorns. Believe me, I wouldn't try it again for a mint of money. I just kept on until by the time I realized how silly I was, it would have been worse to go back than to go forward.

"Don't sit there blinking like an owl, Arvid. Get me some bandage and iodine. If I'm not scarred for life, it will be a miracle. I feel as if I had had a battle with a tiger. A big knot got me across the face and nearly did for me. And then it was a good three-mile walk around the bay after I struck the trail. As for stones—say, boys, I am going to stake out a combination quarry and gravel-pit on that trail some day.

When I staggered through that doorway just now, it was the happiest thing I ever did in my life."

I watched the two reflectively, while Arvid, not suffering from a torn foot, as I was, busied himself helping John.

"If you really had drowned, John," I remarked, "we would have put the pole-star on trial for murder."

"Or the witch at the circus, for scaring you to death," said Arvid.

"The prosecution would have failed, in either case," said John, "for you are both wrong. I myself should have been the one to be prosecuted, for being a superstitious fool."

Suddenly John laughed and Arvid joined in. As the two worked over John's cuts and scratches, I felt all at once free from the uncanny influence that had so strangely affected our lives that evening, and I knew that the others felt as I did.

THE CLOSING HAND

Weird Tales, March 1923

Solitary and forbidding, the house stared specterlike through scraggly trees that seemed to shrink from its touch.

The green moss of decay lay on its dank roofs, and the windows, set in deep cavities, peered blindly at the world as if through eyeless sockets. So forbidding was its aspect that boys, on approaching its cheerless gables, stopped their whistling and passed on the opposite side of the street.

Across the fields, a few huddled cottages gazed through the falling rain, as if wondering what family could be so bold as to take up its abode within the gloomy walls of that old mansion, whose carpetless floors for two years had not felt the tread of human feet.

In an attic room of the house two sisters lay in bed, but not asleep. The younger sister cringed under the dread inspired by the bleak place. The elder laughed at her childish fears, but the younger felt the spell of the old building and was afraid.

"I suppose there is really nothing to frighten me in this dreary old house," she admitted, without conviction in her voice, "but the very feel of the place is horrible. Mother shouldn't have left us alone in this gruesome place."

"Stupid," her sister scolded, "with all the silverware downstairs, somebody has to be here, for fear of burglars."

"Oh, don't talk about burglars!" pleaded the younger girl. "I am afraid. I keep imagining I hear ghostly footsteps."

Her sister laughed.

"Go to sleep, Goosie," she said. "'Haunted' houses are

nothing but superstition. They exist only in imagination."

"Why has nobody lived here for two years, then? They tell me that for five years every family moved out after being here just a short time. The whole atmosphere of the house is ghastly. And I can't forget how the older Berkheim girl was found stabbed to death in her bed, and nobody ever knew how it happened. Why, she may have been murdered in this very room!"

"Go to sleep and don't scare yourself with such silly talk. Mother will be with us tomorrow night, and Dad will be back next day. Now go to sleep."

The elder sister soon dropped into slumber, but the younger lay open-eyed, staring into the black room and shuddering at every stifled scream of the wind or distant growl of thunder. She began to count, hoping to hypnotize herself into drowsiness, but at every slight noise she started, and lost her count.

Suddenly she turned and shook her sister by the shoulder.

"Edith, somebody is prowling around downstairs!" she whispered. "Listen! Oh, what shall we do?"

The elder sister struck a match and lit the candle. Then she slipped on her dressing-gown, and drew on her slippers

"You're not going down there? Edith, tell me you're not going downstairs! It might be that murdered Berkheim girl! Edith, don't—"

Edith shot a glance of withering scorn at her sister, who lay on the bed with blanched face and wide, terrified eyes.

"There is something moving around downstairs, and I'm going to find out what it is," she said.

Taking the candle, she left the room. Her younger sister lay in the darkness, listening to the pattering of rain on the roof and straining her ears to catch the slightest sound. The noise downstairs ceased, but the wind rose and the rain beat upon the roof in sudden furious blasts that made her heart jump wildly. . . . .

Ten minutes passed—twenty minutes—and Edith had not returned.

A door slammed, and the younger sister thought she heard something moving again, but the wind began to sob and drowned out all other noises. Between gusts, she heard the portentous sound, and each time it seemed nearer.

Then—she started as she realized that something was coming up the stairs. Once she thought she heard a cry, to which the wind joined its plaintive voice in a weird duet.

Nearer and nearer the strange noise came. It mounted the stairs, step by step, heard only when the wind and rain softened their voices. It passed the first landing, and moved slowly up the second flight, while the girl fearfully awaited its coming.

The wind howled until the house quaked; it shrilled past the eaves and fled across the fields like a hunted ghost.

And now the girl's pounding pulses drowned out the screaming of the wind, for the presence had *invaded her bedroom!*

She cowered under the covers, a cold perspiration chilling her body until her teeth chattered. Her imagination conjured up frightful things—a disembodied spirit come to destroy her—a corpse from the grave, gibbering in terror because it could not tear the cerements from it face—the murdered Berkheim girl, with the knife still sheathed in her heart—or some escaped beast, licking its lips in greedy anticipation of the feast her tremulous body would provide. Or was it a murderer, who having killed her sister, was now bent on completing his bloody work?

A flash of lightning split the sky, and the thunder bellowed its terrifying warning. The girl threw back the bedclothes and shrank to the wall, her eyes starting from their sockets, fearful lest another flash reveal some sight too ghastly to contemplate.

Slowly the being dragged itself across the floor, lifted itself onto the bed, and uttered a choking sound of agony.

The girl sat petrified. Then, timorously, she extended a shaky hand, but quickly withdrew it in dread of some hideous contact.

Again she thrust her trembling hand into the gloom, farther, farther, until it touched something shaggy and wet.

A clammy hand closed over hers, and she started to her feet, with a horrified scream.

The icy hand tightened with a sickening tremor, and dragged her down. Then her tortured senses gave way, and she fell back unconscious upon the bed. . . . .

When she awoke, it was day. Beside her, on the bed, lay the bleeding body of her sister, Edith, stabbed in the breast by the burglar she had tried to frighten away.

The younger girl was clutching the clotted wisps of hair that had fallen across the breast of her sister, whose cold hand had closed over hers in the last convulsive shudder of death.

THE SNAKE FIEND

Weird Tales, April 1923

Even as a child, Jack Crimi delighted in collecting reptiles, and he seemed to absorb much of their venomous nature.

His best-loved pet was a large blacksnake; but when it caused him a whipping by crawling into his father's bedroom, he roasted it over a slow fire in a large pot, listening with glee to its agonized hissing and pushing it back with a stick when it strove to crawl out of the searing container. It is no cause for wonder, then, that his burning love for the girl of his dreams turned to fierce hate when she became the bride of another.

Crimi's sentiment for Marjorie Bressi was aroused by her fine Italian beauty, which reminded him of his mother. He could have fallen in love with any other girl as easily, if he had set his mind to it in the same way. By dint of comparing her with his mother's picture, he conceived a great admiration for her: then he wished to possess her, to be her lord and master, to marry her. Gazing on her every day with this thought in his mind, his admiration grew to a burning passion. Of all this he said nothing to Marjorie, and then it was too late.

Marjorie loved, and was loved by, Allen Jimerson, a young civil engineer. Crimi neither threatened nor cajoled. He simply accepted the fact, and meditated revenge. He was all smiles at their wedding, and he gave them a wedding present beyond what he could reasonably afford, while he planned to tumble their happiness in ruins about their ears.

After a short honeymoon, Jimerson departed with his

wife to take up his duties as resident engineer of some construction work on a western railroad. Crimi, his face glowing with friendship and good will, was the last to clasp Marjorie's hand in farewell, as the train pulled out of the station.

"Write to me often, Marjorie," was his parting injunction. "Send me a letter as soon as you get settled, and let me know how you are getting along. I don't want to lose touch with either of you."

And he meant it.

Marjorie was fond of the handsome, manly-looking Italian youth, and liked him immensely as a friend, although she had never been in love with him. No sooner was she settled in her new home than she wrote him a long letter, telling of her husband's work, the bleakness of the desert country, and the strange newness of her life. She and her husband occupied a cabin together, apart from the bunk-houses of the construction camp, in the sagebrush region of northern California, not far from the Nevada border.

A fierce joy and exultation leapt in Crimi's heart as he read Marjorie's letter.

"You would like the country better than I do," she wrote, "for it is infested with rattlesnakes. The bare desert rocks on the ridge four miles from our cabin are swarming with them. Ugh! They sun themselves in tangled masses, Allen says, but truly I can't bring myself to go near the place. I get quite too much of snakes without that, for we are constantly killing them in the sagebrush. This country has never been settled, and except for an occasional prospector, there was nobody to kill them before the surveyors came.

The Indians never bother the snakes, but pass by on the other side of a sage-brush and leave them in peace."

Crimi scored these lines in red ink, word by word, as if to blazon them on his memory, and he drew little pictures of snakes on the margin. He burned out Marjorie's signature with acid, spitefully watching with minute care as the letters faded, and gleaning a savage satisfaction from seeing the paper rot away under the venomous bite of the poison. Then he fed the letter to the flames, as he had roasted his blacksnake, years before, and watched the missive burn into black ashes and crumble slowly away, page by page, into gray dust.

Followed Crimi's pursuit of the pair. His arrival was not expected by either Jimerson or Marjorie, but it was none the less welcome, for both of them liked the genial, companionable Italian. Life on the edge of the desert had few distractions at best. Crimi's eyes lit with genuine pleasure at sight of his prospective victims. The joy on both sides was sincere.

"No, this isn't a pleasure trip," he explained to them, "although I expect to have pleasure enough out of it before I get through. I have turned from collecting reptiles to studying their lives and habits. I intend to write a monograph on rattlesnakes. When I got your letter, Marjorie, I knew that I could do no better than to come here. I expect to become very well acquainted with that ridge you wrote about, where the snakes sun themselves in tangled masses."

Marjorie shuddered, and Crimi laughed.

"Well, don't bring any of your snakes around here," she said. "I turn cold and something grips at my insides every time I hear one rattle."

Crimi built himself a small cabin about a mile from the Jimersons, in the direction of the rattlesnake ridge. He adorned the shack tastefully, and Marjorie's deft hand gave a distinctly feminine neatness and charm to its appearance.

He became a frequent visitor at the Jimerson cabin, and evening after evening he read to them in his melodious, well modulated voice. Sometimes the draughtsman or transitman would come in, and Crimi would join in playing cards until late at night.

He seemed to take keen pleasure in the company of Marjorie and her husband, and his face always lit up at sight of them, especially when they were together. But it was the joy of a boy who sees the apples ripening for him on his neighbor's tree, and knows that they will soon be ready for him to pluck. He was most happy when he was meditating his frightful revenge. As his preparations drew near their end, he often spent whole hours gloating over the fate in store for the couple. For Marjorie, in loving Jimerson, had aroused him to insane jealousy, and Jimerson, having robbed him of his heart's desire, was included in Crimi's fierce hate for the girl who had crossed him.

When, one evening, Marjorie and her husband happened in at Crimi's cabin, Marjorie expressed her horror at the thought of Crimi wandering among the snake-infested rocks of the rattlesnake ridge. The snake-hunter seated her on a box that contained a twisting knot of the venomous reptiles.

Marjorie, serenely unaware, talked on blithely, and Crimi's merry laugh pealed out at regular intervals. He was in right jovial mood that evening, for he was ready to spring the death-trap prepared for his two friends. He only awaited a favorable opportunity to strike.

The opportunity came when the surveyors' cook, crazed by bad whisky, smashed up the kitchen. Jimerson discharged him, and the cook muttered threats of a horrible vengeance.

"Shut up," Jimerson ordered. "This is the third time you've been seeing snakes, and now you've wrecked the cook shack. You ought to be sent to jail—or a lunatic asylum."

"It's *you* that will be seeing snakes," the cook splattered. "You an' that Italian wife of yours 'll see plenty of 'em—red, an' green, an'—"

Jimerson struck him across the mouth and sent him on his way. This was in the evening. The draughtsman and rodman went to town the next day to hire a new cook, while Jimerson and Marjorie went on an outing up the headwaters of Feather Creek. It was Sunday, and they intended to spend the day there.

Crimi declined their invitation to accompany them. It was the moulting season, he explained, when the snakes were casting their skins. He could ill afford to lose a day of observation at this time, for he had several perplexing points to clear up before writing his monograph.

Crimi walked fearlessly from rock to rock of the rattlesnake ridge, chuckling to himself. The tangled masses of snakes, of which he had been told, existed only in rumor, although there were snakes in plenty if one but looked for them. Tangled masses would serve his purpose later, but he had gathered them here and there, one or two at a time.

By noon the little cluster of cabins occupied by the engineers was deserted. Marjorie and her husband had been gone since sun-up, and the surveyors were all in town. Not a soul was stirring in the neighborhood of the shacks, and the men at the construction camp were mostly lying around in their bunks, or playing cards.

Crimi nailed fast the windows of Jimerson's cabin. Then he entered and secured the bed to the floor so that it could not be moved. He laboriously carried his boxes of snakes a mile or more, from his room to the little gully behind the surveyors' cabins, and hid them in the sagebrush.

Marjorie and her husband came back from their tramp after dark that evening, dog-tired. Marjorie cooked a little supper, and by 10 o'clock the two were asleep. Crimi entered their cabin about midnight. They were fast in the chains of slumber, and he did not even find it necessary to muffle his tread. He removed the chairs, shoes, clothes, and even the hand mirror and toilet articles. Everything that might serve as a weapon, no matter how slight, he took away.

Then he brought his snakes from the gully, and collected them in front of the cabin. When he had assembled them all, he knocked the top from the largest box, carried it into the room, and, in the audacity of his certain triumph, he dumped the twisting mass of rattlesnakes on the bed where Marjorie and her husband lay asleep.

The other boxes he emptied quickly just inside of the door, and withdrew, for he had no wish to set foot among the venomous serpents. Revenge is never satisfied if retribution overtakes the avenger, and Crimi had no wish to share the fate of his victims. He locked the door from the outside, and battened it. Then he removed the boxes that had contained the snakes, and returned to his cabin and peacefully went to sleep.

Marjorie awoke with the first rays of the sun, and lazily opened her eyes.

Her heart leapt suddenly into her throat, and she was wide awake in an instant. The flat, squat head of a rattlesnake was creeping along her breast. Its beady eyes were fixed on her face, and its red tongue flickered before her like a forked flame. For a moment she thought she was still dreaming, but the familiar outlines of the room limned themselves in her consciousness, and she knew that what she saw was real.

Her shriek rent the air, as she threw back the bed clothes and sprang to the floor. She stepped on a coiled serpent, which sounded an ominous warning as it struck out blindly.

She quickly climbed back on the bed, and stood on the pillow, screaming. Her husband was beside her at once, hazily trying to understand the import of the hysterical torrent of words she was sobbing into his ears. For an instant he thought she must be in the clutch of some horrible nightmare. Then a quick, startled glance around the room turned his blood to ice.

There was now a continuous rattling, as of dry leaves blowing against a stone wall, for Marjorie's screams had galvanized the snakes into activity. The room was filled with their angry din. It sounded in Jimerson's ears like the crack of doom. The floor seemed covered with the creeping reptiles. Some were coiled, the whirring tips of their tails making an indistinct blur as they rattled, and their heads swaying slowly back and forth. Others writhed along the floor, their venomous squat heads thrusting forward and withdrawing, and their tongues darting out like red flames.

On the bed itself there was motion underneath the thrown-back coverlet, and the ugly, gray head of a thick, four-foot snake protruded from under it, its evil eyes shining dully, as if through a film of dust. It extricated itself, and coiled as if to strike, while Marjorie shrank fearfully against the wall, wide-eyed with horror.

Jimerson attacked the reptile with a pillow, sweeping it from the bed onto the floor. He quickly looked about him for a weapon, and saw at once that he was trapped. There was not even a shoe or a pincushion with which to fight the crawling, rattling creatures.

He tried to rock the bed toward the window, as boys move saw-horses forward while sitting on them. But the bed was firmly fastened to the floor, and in his efforts to release it he was bitten on the wrist by the strike of a large snake coiled near the foot of the bed.

Jimerson flung the reptile across the room, and sprang to the floor with an oath, crushing a large rattler with his heel as he jumped. He raced to the door, and wrestled with it for a full minute before he discovered that he and Marjorie were locked in that serpent-hole.

He sprang to the window, and felt a sharp stab of pain in the flesh of his calf as the open jaws of another reptile found their mark, and the poison fangs were imbedded deep in the flesh. The window, like the door, was nailed fast, but he broke out the glass with his bare fists.

Unmindful of the blood on his lacerated hands, he was back at the bedside, treading over reptiles with his bare feet. Marjorie lay on the bed, unconscious.

He lifted her in his bleeding arms and hurled her through the window to safety. He struggled out after her, tearing open his bitten leg on the jagged pieces of glass still left in the window frame. The spurting blood drenched him, and he leaned, faint and dizzy, against the cabin as three of his surveyors came running up, having been attracted by Marjorie's screams.

In almost incoherent words he told them what had happened. He asked them to make immediate search for the discharged cook, for there was no doubt in Jimerson's mind that it was the cook who had placed the snakes in the room.

Then the sky went suddenly black before his eyes, and he lost consciousness.

At that minute Crimi was waking from peaceful dreams. He recalled what he had done the night before, and blissfully mused on what must be taking place in the Jimerson cabin.

A phantasmagoric succession of pictures weltered in his mind—Marjorie and her husband fighting with bare hands against the serpents—bitten a score of times by the angry fangs of the rattlesnakes—clinging to each other in terror—sinking to the floor in agony as the poison swelled their tortured limbs and overcame them—lying green and blue in death, with rattlesnakes crawling and hissing over their dead bodies.

It is remarkable how few people die from rattlesnake bites even when as badly bitten as Jimerson was. Probably not one adult victim in a hundred succumbs to the venom, although mistaken popular belief considers rattlesnake poison as fatal as the death-potion of the Borgias.

Jimerson had known too many cases of snake bite to believe his case hopeless. He did not give up and die, nor did he try to poison his system with whisky. He knew that his condition was serious but he let rest and permanganate of potash, rubbed into his wounds, effect a cure. The bleeding from the lacerated leg had almost entirely washed out the poison, and there was little swelling. The pain of his swollen wrist, however, distended almost to bursting, kept him from sleeping, and the sickly green hue of the bite distressed him. But it did not kill him.

Crimi, careful observer of reptiles though he was, had never known an actual case of snake bite, and he shared the popular illusion that the bite of the rattlesnake dooms its victim to death. Hence he was certain of the complete success of his revenge, and his gloating glee was unclouded by even the shadow of a doubt that Marjorie and her husband had been killed in his death-trap. He awaited only the supreme joy of drinking in the details of his success, to feel the exultant thrill of complete victory.

As Crimi sat alone, two days after that horrible morning, Jimerson was limping slowly toward his cabin. His swollen hand still pained him badly, and there was a dull ache in his ankle when he put too much weight on it, but he thought the fresh air would benefit him.

Supporting himself with a cane, and leaning heavily on Marjorie at times, he went painfully toward the young Italian's desert home. Not once had his suspicion pointed toward Crimi as author of the crime, for the guilt of the lunatic cook seemed all too clear. Besides, he liked Crimi for his genial camaraderie, his joviality and good humor, and his frank interest in everything that concerned either him or Marjorie.

So intent was the snake fiend on passing the torments of his victims before his fancy, that he did not hear the knock on his cabin door. His brain was too busy to heed the message sent by his ears, for he was feasting on the mental and physical tortures that Jimerson and Marjorie must have endured before they lay cold in death on the floor of the cabin, hideously discolored by the venom of the rattlesnakes.

By degrees he became conscious that he was not alone. Two persons stood before him, and he raised his eyes in eager anticipation, to feed his revengeful spirit on the story he had waited two days to hear.

Even when he gazed on those whom he had consigned to a horrible death, the thought that they were alive did not penetrate his consciousness. The idea of failure had never entered his mind for even an instant. They were dead, beyond the peradventure of a doubt, and now—*their avenging ghosts stood before him!*

Crimi dropped to his knees in white terror and crawled behind his chair. He clasped and unclasped his hands in agony of fear. Sweat poured from his face and bathed his body. He implored mercy. He screamed for forgiveness. He gibbered like a frightened ape. Half forgotten words of Italian, learned at his mother's knee, fell from his lips. He pleaded and begged for his life, crawling on his face toward the amazed couple in an endeavor to clasp their knees.

As the meaning of his broken ejaculations was borne in on them, a tremendous loathing and disgust overcame them. Marjorie clung to her husband, unnerved at the repulsive sight of the malicious coward groveling on the floor and trying to kiss their feet.

Crimi shrieked and gnawed his hands as he saw the avenging angels of his victims leave the cabin.

It was impossible for the stern hand of the law to inflict a greater punishment on Jack Crimi than his own malice had wrought for him. Today he occupies a padded cell in a hospital for the incurably insane.

THE TEAK-WOOD SHRINE

Weird Tales, September 1923

Here ends the curse of the teak-wood devil. Its tale of horror is full. I have brought it here to this bridge to throw it into the river before it brings more misery into the world.

I don't wonder that you look amazed at me, sir, for I am much changed since you last saw me, a scant two months ago. I am no longer the same woman, for the power of the teak-wood shrine has dragged me through hell. See how the teak-wood devil grins! How the little rubies of its eyes shine! Do you think it does not know what it has done to me—that it is merely a dead thing of wood and precious stones? It knows only too well. It has turned my hair white and lined my face with suffering. I have forgotten how to smile.

Oh, no, sir, I would rather you did not take it into your hands. Let me hurl it over the railing. Let me destroy it at once. No, I beseech you, sir! Not for all the wealth of the world would I give this jeweled shrine away. It can cause nothing but unhappiness and troubled thoughts—thoughts so terrible that only death can chase them away.

No person has ever looked into this shrine and lived, save only me and one other—but he was a holy man of India, and I am dying. My sands are running out rapidly. I shall welcome death.

This is the Shrine-devil. See how sleek and yellow it is! How fat and smiling! Was it carved thus, think you, to quell suspicion and invite the unfortunate possessor to touch the ruby that opens the sliding door? How unctuously that little idol guards its terrible secret!

A thousand dollars? No, sir, not for fifty thousand would I sell it to you, nor for fifty times fifty thousand. Money cannot buy happiness for me. But grief and suffering would attend you if I gave you this shrine. The secret locked in its heart would drive you mad. If death failed to hunt you out, you would go in search of it. For the secret is not to be borne. I have looked into the shrine and I still live, but that is because of my prayers before I touched the jewel that released the little panel. Woe is me that I prayed! For had I not prayed, I might now be dead, and therefore happy, instead of slowly drowning in the welter of misery that rises ever higher about me.

A holy man of India gave the shrine to a Christian bishop who had done him a great service.

"Ask and you shall receive," he said; but he fell upon his knees and begged release from his promise when the bishop demanded this little teak-wood shrine.

"The bishop knows not what he asks," said the holy man. "Fain would I grant him anything but this, for it will bring him misery and ruin."

"Nay, by my holy faith," said the bishop, "since you have asked me to choose, and it is no small service I have done you, I will be satisfied with nothing else but the shrine. I shall annul the power of the shrine-devil with a Christian prayer, and show you once more the impotency of pagan charms."

"Bishop, bishop," answered the holy man very gravely, "it will take a potent spell indeed to chain the fat devil of the teak-wood shrine. And until you find that potent spell, I conjure you not to examine the shrine too closely, lest you touch by chance the little jewel push-button that opens the door to the mystery within it, for then you will be lost utterly."

"Tonight," said the bishop, "I shall open it."

"Nay," said the holy man, "if I thought you were not jesting, I would kill you now, and count myself your benefactor as having saved you from misery the like of which you cannot dream exists."

So the bishop gave his promise that he would not open the shrine. For months the teak-wood devil smiled at him from behind the big Bible in his study and wrought him no manner of harm at all, for he had not pressed the ruby that opens the sliding door.

Then one day guests came to the bishop's house, and he told them the story of the shrine, even as I have related it to you. One of them took it into his hands and curiously examined the jewels that were embedded in the teak. As he examined it, his face turned ghastly pale, and he stared like a man whose eyes are fixed open in death, for by chance he had touched the ruby and opened the sliding door.

Then he uttered a laugh so mirthless, so terrible, that one of the women shrieked and fainted dead away. It was plain that the man was a maniac.

The bishop took from his hands the shrine, and touched in his turn the revealing ruby. The panel slid back again, and the bishop found himself looking into the interior of the shrine.

"There is nothing here at all," he exclaimed, "but McRae has gone mad from terror."

Then suddenly the bishop's face went white, as he realized what he had seen. He sank to his knees and prayed. McRae broke away from the group and ran to his lodgings in the English quarter of that native village. When they went for him he lay dead on the floor, grasping tightly in his hand the revolver with which he had slain himself. The bishop never ceased to cry out for death, and he passed away in delirium within a week.

There was in the bishop's household a native servant, who had listened to his master's recital and witnessed the tragic results of opening the shrine. He determined to possess the treasure, because of the jewels that shone between the yellow hands of the image. The servant was very cautious, for he feared lest he might himself experience the agony of soul that had killed the bishop and caused McRae to slay himself. He visited a seer, therefore, and paid ten rupees for a spell to bind the teak-wood devil. Then the servant took the shrine from the bishop's study, and fled with it to Singapore, where he tried to dispose of it. But the shops all turned against him, and offered him little or nothing for his treasure, for they said the jewels were of no value.

Disconsolate, the servant took the shrine between his knees and tried to dig out the rubies that lay between the hands of the guardian image, for he thought they must be large and perfect. Inadvertently, he touched the ruby push-button, and the panel slid back for an instant, and he saw the mystery.

His heart was troubled, but he did not understand what he had seen. This was because of the spell put upon him by the seer. Because he had not understood, he explored the mystery again, and the door slid back a second time. And now he knew.

The power of the incantation was exhausted, for it was purchased with stolen rupees. A veil fell away from the servant's eyes, and he saw into the shrine with a clear brain and full understanding of what he looked upon. He knew now why poor McRae had killed himself, and why the bishop had prayed for death.

Concealing the shrine in a fold of his sash, the servant went down to the water-front to cast it away. He stood on the wharf and watched a liner about to move away across the ocean. A great envy fell upon him of all those people, because they were ignorant of the secret hidden in the shrine, and could therefore still be happy. With this envy came also a great wave of self-pity, for the teak-wood devil was scourging his brain, and he knew that he could never smile again.

Then he took the terrible thing from his sash, to throw it into the sea. The jewels that were the eyes of the teak-wood image threw out a strange light, and an American, hurrying to board the ship, stopped with a shrill whistle, and demanded to see the curious object. The servant refused, but the American persisted, and offered much money for the treasure. The man shook his head sadly, and told the American the whole history of the shrine, as he had heard it from the bishop, even as I have repeated it to you.

The American forced into the servant's hands a roll of bills, and rushed up the gang-plank with the shrine in his arms, for the men on the ship were calling to him. The servant waved the bills at him frantically, and struggled to follow him, but the deck-hands stopped him, the gang-plank was pulled up, and the liner moved slowly away.

The American dived into his stateroom and concealed the object in the covers of his berth. Then he returned to the deck. A crowd was gathered on the dock, and there was a great commotion, but of the bishop's servant there was no sign. He had jumped into the sea.

The American was John Aubrey, my late master, who first told me the story of the shrine on his return from India. He told me the tale again two months ago, with madness gleaming from his eyes, and begged me to destroy the thing, to throw it into the river, to let it sink where human eyes would nevermore look upon it.

You were my master's friend, and to you I can talk. It was this teak-wood shrine that killed him. He took it from the mantel to show it to me. Disbelieving its power, disbelieving the entire story told him by the bishop's servant at Singapore—for he had been unable to find the hidden spring of the shrine—he suddenly, by an evil chance, pressed the ruby, and the panel slid open. He tried to prevent it from closing, and inserted the nail of his little finger, but the door slid back into place notwithstanding, after he had caught a fleeting glimpse into the very heart of the shrine.

He laughed triumphantly to think he had at last found the touch-button. He was as excited as a small boy over his discovery. That was because he did not yet know what he had seen. But soon he began to worry, and his face grew slowly more and more drawn, as the terrible truth began to take hold of his brain. His eyes filled with dread. His brows contracted in horror. He made me promise to destroy the shrine. Then he went to his room and locked the door.

I concealed the object, which I now hated with all my soul, for I wanted no more misery brought into the world by its hideous means. I was called at the inquest, with the other servants, but I told only what the others told, about how we heard the shot, and broke open the door, and found our master lying dead on the floor of his bedroom. But of the teak-wood shrine, and the hidden panel, and the fat devil with the wooden belly and the ruby eyes, I said not a word to anybody.

And then I prayed—God, how I prayed!—that unto me it might be given to release the world from this horror. Then I touched the ruby and saw what it was that the teak-wood image was guarding so complacently. It is because of my prayers that I am undergoing this life in death, this burden of misery, instead of being happy in the grave.

It must be in answer to my prayers that today I have the strength to bring the shrine to this bridge to throw it into the muddy waters. When that is done I shall be ready to die. My life is ebbing, and I am moving swiftly to my grave. I have read the teak-wood devil's secret, and all the sweetness and light have gone from my life.

Give me back the shrine, sir, or else fling it with your own hands, at once and forever, into the blessed depths of the water. No, no, sir, you must not look for the jewel! At once, fling it, or you will be yourself its victim!

Oh, oh! You have done it! You have looked!—

What horrid sound is that?—You laugh, but that is because you do not yet know.—Now, do you begin to realize?—You know now what I have suffered. You have entered upon the path that can end only in death.

Oh, oh, oh!—Help me, you at the end of the bridge— Oh, gentlemen, hurry!—That is where they sank!—Look, they are going down for the third time! They are lost, they are gone! He and the teak-wood devil! Heaven be thanked!

And now, sirs, you may take me away—to a hospital, or an asylum for the insane. It matters not where, for my days are numbered. Nothing matters any more, for the curse of the teak-wood devil is ended. Good sirs, take me away.

AN ADVENTURE IN THE FOURTH DIMENSION

Weird Tales, October 1923

The thought of meteors terrifies me. They have a disagreeable habit of coming down and killing people at the most inopportune times. That is why I was so startled when I saw a large object hurtling toward me out of the sky, as I was walking along the lake front recently in my city of Chicago.

I shivered. Was this the end? I began to say my prayers. To my astonishment, the onrushing missile struck the grass beside me without the slightest jar.

I gasped.

Thousands of singular objects began to detach themselves. They bounded from the mass, and suddenly increased in size from one inch to three feet in diameter. They were entirely round, and covered with teeth. On each tooth were ten ears, constantly in motion. Each ear carried a quizzical eye.

The dwarfish creatures rolled rapidly on the ground, the ears serving as legs, hands, tentacles and what not, propelling them with incredible speed. Sometimes they stood on only four or five of their ears, then suddenly pressed hard against the ground with half a thousand ears at once, thus bounding high into the air. They lit without jar, for the ears acted as shock absorbers and broke their fall.

"Surely these are explorers from Mars or Venus," I thought, as the funny bounding creatures filled the air.

"You are wrong. They are Jupiterians," said a voice beside me.

I recognized the voice. It was Professor Nutt. You probably know him.

"Ahem," he said. "Ahem, ahem!" And once more he repeated, "Ahem!"

"Interesting, if true," I remarked. "And what might Jupiterians be?"

"They might be men, but they're not," he snapped. "They are people from the planet Jupiter. Out of your ignorance you thought they might be Martians or Venusians, but you are wrong, for Mars and Venus have people of three dimensions, like ourselves. Jupiterians are entirely different. There are six hundred thousand of them in this Jupiterian airship."

I was so overjoyed at finding someone who could tell me about them, that I didn't think to ask him how he knew all these startling facts.

"Where is the airship you speak of?" I asked.

"There it is," he answered, rather grandiloquently, and pointed to an empty spot on the grass.

I looked carefully, and made out a vast, transparent globe, apparently of glass, which was rapidly becoming visible because of the Chicago dust that was settling upon it. I approached, and touched it with my hand. It gave forth a metallic ring.

"Aha," laughed the professor. "You thought it was glass, but it is made of Jupiterian steel. Look out!"

I sprang back at his warning, and the last hundred thousand leapt out of the globe, passing right through the transparent metal of which it was composed.

"Nom de mademoiselle!" I exclaimed, in astonishment.

This was a swear word I had learned in France when I was in the army.

"Nom de mademoiselle!" I repeated, for I liked to show off my knowledge of the language. "How can they pass through the glass without breaking it?"

"Through the Jupiterian steel, you mean," said Professor Nutt, severely. "I told you before that it is not glass. Jupiterian steel has four dimensions, and they pass through the fourth dimension. That is why you can't see the metal, for your eyes are only three-dimensional."

"Are the Jupiterian people four-dimensional?" I asked, awed.

"Certainly," said Nutt, rather irritably.

"Then how is it that I can see them?" I exclaimed triumphantly.

"You see only three of their four dimensions," he replied. "The other one is inside."

I turned to look again at the Jupiterians, who now covered the whole waterfront. One of them sprang lightly, fifty feet into the air, extended a hundred ears like tentacles, and seized an English sparrow. He crushed the sparrow with some score or more of his teeth, which, as I have said, covered his whole body. In less than a minute the poor bird was chewed to pieces. I looked closer, and saw that the Jupiterian had no mouth.

"Nom de mademoiselle!" I exclaimed, for the third time. "How can it get the bird into its stomach?"

"Through the fourth dimension," said Professor Nutt.

It was true. The chewed-up pieces of the bird were suddenly tossed into the air, and the Jupiterian sprang lightly after them. In mid-air he turned inside out, caught the pieces of the bird in his stomach, and lit on the grass

again right side up with care.

"Did you see that?" I exclaimed, in a hushed voice. "Why can't I turn inside out that way?"

"Because you are not four-dimensional," replied the professor, a trace of annoyance in his voice. "It is a beautiful thing to have four dimensions," he rhapsodized. "Your Jupiterian is your only true intellectual, for he alone can truly reflect. He turns his gaze in upon himself."

"And sees what he had for breakfast?" I gasped. "And what his neighbors had, too?"

"Your questions are childish," said the professor, wearily. "A Jupiterian, of course, can look into the soul of things, and see what his neighbors had for breakfast, as you so vulgarly express it. But Jupiterians turn their thoughts to higher things."

The creatures now surrounded me, their ears turned inwards, as if they were supplicating.

"What do they want?" I asked the professor.

"They want something to drink," he replied. "They are pointing their ears toward their stomachs to show that they are thirsty."

"Oh," I said, and pointed toward the lake. "There is the fresh cool water of the lake, if they are thirsty."

"Don't be fantastic," said Professor Nutt. "It isn't water they want."

He fixed his stern, pitiless gaze on my hip pocket. I turned pale, for it was my last pint. But I had to submit. If you have ever had Professor Nutt's cold, accusing eyes on you, you will know just how I felt.

I drew the flask from my pocket, and handed it to the chief Jupiterian, who waggled his ears in joy. Immediately there was pandemonium, if you know what I mean. Ten thousand times ten thousand ears seized the cork, and pulled it out with a resounding pop. One thirsty Jupiterian passed right through the glass into the bottle in his eagerness to get at the contents, and nearly drowned for his pains.

"You see how useful it is to be four-dimensional," remarked the professor. "You could get into any cellar in the world by merely passing through the walls. And into any beer-keg in the same way."

"But," I argued, "how did this—this insect get through the glass into the whisky bottle? Glass has only three dimensions, like everything else in this world."

"Don't call him an insect!" Nutt sharply reprimanded me. "He is a Jupiterian, and as such he is infinitely superior to you and me. He passed through the glass because he is four-dimensional, even though the glass isn't. If you had four dimensions, you could untie any knot by merely passing it through itself. You could turn inside out, or pass through yourself until your right hand became your left hand, and change into your own image as you see it in the looking-glass."

"Nom de mademoiselle!" I exclaimed, for the fourth time.

A distant noise of barking was borne to my ears by the breeze. All the dogs in the city seemed to have gone wild.

"They are disturbed by the talking of the Jupiterians," explained the professor. "It is too high-pitched for clodhopper human ears to hear, unless they have an unusual range, but the dogs can hear it plainly."

I listened, and finally made out a very shrill humming, higher than any sound I had ever heard before in my life, and infinitely sweet and piercing.

"Ah, I am hearing four-dimensional sounds," I thought, aloud.

"Wrong, as usual," exacerbated the professor, with much heat. "Sound has no dimensions. It proceeds in waves, and bends back upon itself until it meets itself at an infinite distance from the starting point. There are three reasons why you can't hear the music of the spheres: first, because it is bent away from the earth by the force of gravity as it passes the sun; second, because your ears are not attuned to so shrill a sound; and third, because there *is* no music of the spheres. The first two reasons are really unnecessary, in the light of the third; but a scientific mind such as mine is not content with one reason when three can be adduced just as easily."

"Shades of Sir Oliver Lodge!" I ejaculated.

"Sir Oliver is alive," the professor corrected me. "A man does not become a shade until after his death. Then he becomes a four-dimensional creature like the Jupiterians, only different."

"Nom de mademoiselle!" I commented.

"Say something sensible," he reprimanded me.

"For the love of Einstein, how do you know all these things about the Jupiterians?" I asked, a sudden suspicion flashing across what I am pleased to call my mind.

"Ah, Einstein, yes," exclaimed Nutt, greatly pleased. "My mother's father's name was Einstein."

"Then you are related to—"

"No, I am not related," he interrupted, "but my mother's father is."

"A sort of fourth-dimensional relationship, I suppose," I remarked sarcastically.

At that moment the air became vibrant with an invisible sound. The Jupiterians came rolling from all directions, as if they had suddenly heard the dinner bell. They bounded through the Jupiterian steel of the globe, and immediately shrank in size from three feet to one inch.

"The Jupiterian assembly call just blew," explained the professor. "Notice how the passengers draw into themselves. Six hundred thousand are now packed into that globe. Our elevated railroads miss a great opportunity by not having four-dimensional creatures to deal with."

"They pack us in just as tight," I ventured to remark.

The globe had begun to shoot into the air, when there came from behind me a high-pitched wail of distress, a shriller and higher sound than had ever before been heard by human ears, so the professor assured me. The chief Jupiterian had been left behind. He it was who had passed into the whisky bottle. Not content with getting the lion's share of the contents, he had surrounded the bottle, in his pleasant four-dimensional way, and now he could not get rid of it.

"Why doesn't he turn inside out again, and drop the bottle?" I asked, watching the Jupiterian with interest.

"Because your whisky has paralyzed him," answered the professor. "He is quite helpless."

I looked at the globe, which had alighted again. Each Jupiterian suddenly resumed his full size, in a brave attempt to bound to the assistance of his chief. But the creatures could no longer pass through the four-dimensional metal of which the globe was composed. So thick a layer of Chicago dust had settled upon it, that to all intents and purposes it had become three-dimensional. The sudden impact of six hundred thousand bodies caused it to burst, with a roar as of a hundred peals of thunder exploding simultaneously. The air was filled with dead and dying Jupiterians. A dark cloud settled over the landscape, composed of the flying dust shaken from the Jupiterian globe by the explosion. Long streamers of electric fire shot from the fragments of the airship, and seemed to curve in upon themselves. Everything ran in curves—the darkness, the cloud, the sounds, the shafts of light—as if bent in by the force of gravity.

I put up my hands and fought the cloud that was settling down upon me. I seemed to be covered with falling feathers, when the cloud began to lift. I found myself in my own parlor. The air was full of flying leaves, which I was madly tearing from a book and throwing toward the ceiling. The book was a treatise on the Einstein theory of space, which I had borrowed from a friend that afternoon. I had read nearly a page in it before I fell asleep.

Only twelve men in the whole world understand the Einstein theory, it is said. If I had read the book, I would have been the thirteenth, and that would be unlucky. So it is just as well that it is destroyed. But what excuse am I to give my friend for tearing up his book?

POISONED

Weird Tales, November 1923

It was a trifling quarrel indeed that broke the life-long friendship of Aubrey Charles the lawyer and Aubrey Leclair the apothecary.

"Look for the woman," says the old proverb. It was not a woman that caused the quarrel between the two Aubreys, but it was because of a woman that the breach widened and friendship turned to hate. Thereby the proverb justifies itself once more.

"Board is play, Aubrey," said Charles as Leclair threw down a king upon the first player's ace.

"Don't be a fool, Aubrey," said Leclair. "I meant to play my deuce. Anybody in his right senses would know I would never play my king on your ace."

"Board is play, Aubrey," repeated Charles, with a rising inflection in his voice. "It's not my fault that you play like a dunce."

Leclair threw his cards into the air, seized his hat, opened his mouth as if to speak, then stamped out of the lawyer's office without a word, slamming the door behind him.

There had been petulant outbursts before, due always to Leclair's habit of taking back his cards after he had played them. Charles had frequently vowed to himself that he never would play with Leclair again. But the pair were inseparable, and they were always at it again next day, the apothecary taking back his plays as carelessly as ever.

Leclair stormed out into the street, distressed beyond

measure that Aubrey Charles placed so little value on his friendship as to insist on such an obviously ridiculous play. Aubrey Charles sat in his inner office berating himself for his irritability, and prepared once more to swallow his dignity, as he had done on several occasions before. He had been unreasonable, and he knew it.

"But I was right, the idiot!" he exclaimed aloud, striking the desk in a fury of resentment. "Board is always play. Good God! Must I be always babying him to keep his friendship?"

There the quarrel might have ended, had it not been for Mazie Lennox, who had nursed both Aubreys through the flu and was engaged to marry Aubrey the attorney. Aubrey Charles, ready to unbend and eat humble pie, yet full of his wrongs, pulled the telephone to him to call up the other Aubrey and apologize, when it struck him that the apothecary would hardly have had time to reach his drug store. So he telephoned to Mazie instead.

In lieu, therefore, of a contrite apology over the telephone from Aubrey Charles, the apothecary got a severe dressing down from Mazie Lennox. It was Mazie who called him first, before the attorney got the wire.

"What under the sun did you mean by stamping out of Aubrey's office and scattering your cards all over the place?" she stormed. "Aubrey, I am downright ashamed of you. Have you no more sense than to let a disagreement over a card game lead to a quarrel between you and Aubrey? What on earth was the matter with you?"

"But Aubrey wanted me to throw away my king on his ace," Aubrey the apothecary exclaimed, scandalized.

To the sense of injury that he nursed against Charles was now added a sense of personal outrage because Charles had told Mazie about the quarrel. Leclair did not know that at that very moment the other Aubrey was trying to reach him on the telephone to beg his pardon and repair the breach between them.

"He treated me as if I were a naughty child, and got angry because I didn't want to throw the game to him by letting the wrong play stand. He called me a dunce."

"What if he did?" said Mazie. "I can't let the two best friends I have in the world quarrel. Now listen, Aubrey. I am going to Klickitamas tonight over the week end. You and Aubrey, both of you, are to follow me tomorrow and forget your differences. I simply won't have you quarreling. That's flat."

With that she rang off, leaving Aubrey the apothecary jiggling the telephone and trying to get her back, wiping the perspiration from his brow as he waited for her to answer. But Mazie was on her way over to the office of the other Aubrey to go out with him to dinner before she left for Klickitamas.

Too proud to refuse Mazie's invitation, too angry to call up Aubrey Charles, Aubrey the apothecary arranged to be absent from his drug store over Sunday, and the next noon he took the train for Klickitamas.

A word or two on the telephone from Aubrey the attorney, who was undoubtedly in the wrong, would have applied balm to his hurt feelings and averted all the tragedy that followed.

But Aubrey the lawyer hated to be put in a false light. Dignity to him was a fetish, before which he worshiped. It was his principal stock in trade. There was not in the whole country a man who made a more impressive appearance in court. Always expensively but conservatively dressed, with upright carriage, serious and noble countenance, heightened by a close-cropped mustache that made him look older than he was, he impressed the juries by his very appearance. Even his games of cards with Aubrey the apothecary were always conducted in the lawyer's inner office, for Aubrey Charles did not wish the public to see him in his moments of relaxation, when he stooped to so trivial a pastime as playing cards.

Therefore Aubrey the lawyer, who in the first flush of contrition over the quarrel had sought to call up Aubrey the apothecary, now waited for the apothecary to make the first move toward reconciliation. He would apologize then, but his dignity would be saved if Leclair called him up first. He could not go to Klickitamas. If he telephoned the apothecary and told him this, he knew very well that the apothecary would also stay away from Klickitamas. But it would seem an admission that he feared to leave Mazie with Leclair over the week-end. Would not Leclair think that it was this reason alone that prompted him to call up and apologize? Reasoning thus, Aubrey the lawyer refrained from telephoning to his friend, and Aubrey the apothecary went to Klickitamas alone.

Aubrey Leclair, as the closest friend and confident of the other Aubrey, regarded Mazie as a pal, but nothing closer, for she was the future wife of his friend. He liked Mazie immensely, and used to follow her about the room with his eyes, feasting them on her well-fitting nurse's garb and her mobile mouth and mysterious brown eyes, when he was recovering from the flu. But from the beginning she and the other Aubrey had taken to each other. They had gone together, after the two Aubreys were out of the hospital. Aubrey the apothecary was the third party, the friend of both, and he had accepted the love of his two friends for each other as a matter of course. He was loyal to his friend Aubrey Charles, and glad to see him win so sterling a girl as Mazie.

But that night everything seemed different. The spell of moonlight and the water worked in him a spring madness, and he desired the girl for himself. Her eyes invited confidences, and her tone was one of tender friendship. Her face was near his. The sense of loyalty to his friend—the friend who had injured him—dissolved like one of his own drugs, in the water and the moonlight. His lips met hers. Mazie drew away and laughed, softly, nervously.

"By proxy," she said, "I enjoyed that. Did you give that to me for Aubrey Charles or Aubrey Leclair?"

He had hardly brushed her lips with his own, but the thrill and promise of the slight kiss intoxicated him, and the warmth of her lips heated his blood.

"That may have been for Aubrey Charles," he exclaimed, in a voice half-choked with sudden emotion, "but this is from Aubrey Leclair."

He pressed her tightly to his breast. Again and again he kissed her, on the throat, the lips, the eyes. She did not struggle, but lay limply in his arms, speechless, powerless, amazed by this treachery of her friend to her friend, as in burning words he declared the strength of his own love.

"Not Aubrey Charles, but Aubrey Leclair," he repeated. "I was loyal to Aubrey while he was loyal to me, but he has broken with me for nothing at all. I refuse to yield you to him."

"Aubrey!"

Mazie's voice rang out, at once angry and beseeching.

"Aubrey, do you realize what you are doing?"

She held out her hand in front of his eyes. A large diamond sparkled in the moonlight. Aubrey the lawyer had placed it upon her finger. The sparkle of that betrothal diamond was to Aubrey Leclair like a piece of ice laid across his heart. The spring madness still possessed him, but it had been touched by the rigor of winter.

"Mazie!" he exclaimed.

His voice sounded far away and distant, like some sinister whispering from evil lips.

"Mazie, I cannot let you marry Aubrey Charles! You with your purity, your sweetness! You must not! I have stood by Aubrey, despite my knowledge of certain events he has kept hidden from the world, because a man looks on such lapses quite differently from a woman. Did you ever hear of Lena May?"

Mazie clapped her hand roughly over Aubrey's mouth, as if to silence him. Then she shrank from him, and shook herself free of his embrace.

"Lena May?" she exclaimed, standing up and confronting Aubrey desperately.

Even in the moonlight Aubrey noticed how pale she was.

"What has Lena May to do with Aubrey?"

"Ask him," replied Aubrey Leclair. "He can't deny it. He wouldn't give her fifty dollars each month for the support of her child unless it were true. I have delivered the money to her each month as Aubrey's errand boy, for he wants no checks made out to her, by which he can be blackmailed later on. You are wearing Aubrey's ring, but it is Lena May who should be wearing it."

A strong shiver of revulsion shook Mazie.

"You beast!" she exclaimed. "You filthy beast! And you

call yourself his friend!"

She fled into the house.

Unbending pride on the one hand, resentment and spring madness on the other—the breach was accomplished in the long friendship of the two Aubreys.

Mazie Lennox ceased to wear Aubrey Charles' ring. A year later she was married to Dr. Armitage, who had been a friend of her youth. Both Aubrey Charles and Aubrey Leclair were silent guests at the wedding. Neither had spoken a word to the other since the day when Aubrey Leclair stormed out of Aubrey Charles' office, scattering the cards about the room as he went.

The tall, dignified lawyer had never seemed so frigid and reserved as on that day when his heart's treasure was given to another. The usually jovial apothecary was as unsmiling and reserved as the other Aubrey. His face was a sober mask.

Aubrey Charles the lawyer left immediately after the minister spoke the words that made Dr. Armitage and Mazie Lennox man and wife. Aubrey Leclair the apothecary was even more downcast than the other Aubrey. He had not only lost the girl himself, but his treachery to Aubrey the attorney had lost him the friendship that he valued above anything that had ever come into his life. He felt that he was to blame for the whole tragedy. A senseless quarrel had ruffled the smooth surface of his comradeship with Aubrey Charles, and he, Aubrey Leclair, instead of steering for untroubled waters, had deliberately wrecked the craft of friendship and overturned the boat. He hated the other Aubrey with all the animus of his nature, venomously, with a hate that would stop at nothing. But at this moment he wanted air. He was choking in the festival atmosphere of the wedding, drowning in the whirlpool of his own emotions. He left the house of mirth abruptly, stepped into his car and left the little city behind him.

Racked by his thoughts, tortured by regrets, stung by hatred, he hardly noticed where he went, until he heard his name called. He drew up beside the curb. He found himself in the streets of a city twenty miles from his own. It was a friend, a fellow apothecary, who was calling to him.

Aubrey got out of his car, and wandered arm in arm into the drug store with the friend who had called to him. He welcomed this brief respite from the torment of his thoughts. And here he learned news that smote him first with a pang of conscience, and then made him glow with pleasure. For the apothecary told him, confidentially, that Aubrey the lawyer had bought a strong poison to kill a large dog, or so at least he had told the druggist when he bought it.

"A dog?" exclaimed Aubrey in some surprise.

"A great Dane he has had for several years," explained the druggist. "It has a tumor, he says, and he finds it necessary to kill the dog. I sold the poison to him because he is a close friend of yours. But I wonder he did not go to you."

"Perhaps," Aubrey said, musingly, "perhaps he was afraid I was so much attached to the dog that I would insist on trying to cure it. Much obliged."

"For what?" asked the apothecary.

"For selling the poison to my friend."

Aubrey Leclair had something new to occupy his thoughts as he motored slowly back. Aubrey the lawyer had never possessed a dog. He evidently did not want Aubrey the apothecary to know that he wanted poison, so he came to this other city to get it. He wanted it, then, for himself. He was very despondent, although his face and demeanor in public showed no relaxation from his habitual dignity and reserve.

Aubrey Charles had indeed bought the poison to slay himself, but his sense of dignity prevented him from carrying out his intention. He found it easier to support the pangs of despondency than to let the world peep into his heart at a coroner's inquest. That inevitable scene was enacted in his mind a hundred times. Always it cost him a shudder to picture the curiosity of his little world of acquaintances (for he had no close friends now that Aubrey Leclair had forsaken him) as they learned how Mazie Lennox had cast him aside because of his clandestine affair with Lena May. Aubrey would be dead when these revelations were made, but even his soul must shrink in shamed humiliation when the world saw what a sorry figure he had cut. So he lived with his bitter thoughts, and the poison remained unused in a cupboard of his inner office.

Aubrey Leclair the apothecary, cheated of the suicide of Aubrey Charles, felt that fate had treated him cruelly. Like the lawyer, he had been robbed of his chum and his girl. Even revenge was denied to him. So when a trivial legal matter that involved his interests made it necessary for him to sign certain papers, he went to the office of Aubrey the lawyer to arrange the matter. This visit would give him the opportunity to see for himself just how deeply the lawyer was suffering from their mutual disaster.

No figure of bronze could have been more unbending than Aubrey Charles when Aubrey Leclair entered the lawyer's office, except that this figure opened its mouth and spoke.

"I will not shake hands, Aubrey," said the figure, slowly. "I do not wish to revive old friendships. But because we were once friends, you and I, I will offer you a glass of wine, pre-prohibition vintage."

The figure moved majestically into the inner office. Aubrey the apothecary, imitating the lawyer's lofty reserve, stood with folded arms awaiting his return. Behind the closed door of the inner office the lawyer's haughtiness dropped from him like a mantle. Feverishly he hunted for a white powder he had placed there some weeks before, at the time of Mazie Lennox's marriage to Dr. Armitage. Finding it, he poured it into a wine glass, filled the glass with wine, and poured out another glass for Aubrey.

Returning to the outer office, he placed one glass before Aubrey Leclair. Before himself he carefully put the poisoned glass. His hand shook so that he spilled some of the wine. His brow was damp with perspiration. His icy reserve had melted utterly. Aubrey the apothecary still stood with folded arms. Slowly he shook his head.

"You drink too much, Aubrey," said the apothecary.

"Not for the love of liquor, Aubrey," replied the lawyer, "but to forget sorrow. You have hurt me, Aubrey, but you have hurt yourself equally. Let us drink."

"You began it,' said Aubrey the apothecary, coldly. "I will not drink with you."

"Perhaps the wine is too strong," persisted Aubrey the lawyer. "You are not a drinking man like me. I will get you some water."

Aubrey the apothecary did not answer. The lawyer seemed perplexed and unwilling to leave the room. The apothecary still stood, an icy statue. Anyone knowing the two, knowing the dignified reserve of the lawyer and the genial good-fellowship of the apothecary, would have thought Aubrey Leclair was the lawyer and Aubrey Charles the apothecary. The lawyer suddenly left the outer office and went quickly into the inner room. Aubrey Leclair heard him turn on the tap. In a minute he returned with a pitcher of water and another glass. The apothecary stood with folded arms as before. Apparently the glasses had not been moved, but Aubrey Leclair's face showed a trace of agitation, which seemed to satisfy Aubrey the lawyer.

"No water, please," said Aubrey the apothecary. "I will drink it as it stands."

"To the health of Mazie Lennox!" said Aubrey Charles in ringing tones, looking with a strange expression of shrewdness and triumph at Aubrey the apothecary.

Without an instant's hesitation, he lifted his own glass, clinked it against the glass of Aubrey Leclair, and carried it to his lips. Both men drained the last drop. Aubrey Charles then snapped the stem of his glass, and tossed it into the waste basket.

"And now to business, Aubrey."

The lawyer had resumed his habitual calm. The two men sat down. Aubrey Charles read aloud, very slowly, the paper that he wanted Aubrey Leclair to sign. From time to time he cast a quick glance at the apothecary. Always he found the eyes of the other fixed on his face. He grew nervous at this unwavering stare, and his glances at the apothecary became more frequent. Aubrey Leclair's gaze never faltered.

A sense of impending tragedy held Aubrey Charles in a vise. His face twitched spasmodically. Why was this? He tried to fight off the dreadful doubt that clutched him. He reasoned with himself thus: Aubrey Leclair has changed the wine glasses, thereby taking for himself the poisoned glass. He thinks that I gave him the poisoned glass, and that he has given it back to me. If it were not so, why would he watch me thus? He is looking for symptoms of poisoning. But it is he who has drunk the poison. Why should I be afraid?

Again his face twitched. He sprang to his feet. A sharp pain shot through his heart. He saw Aubrey the apothecary relax from his intense stare and settle back in his chair, satisfied. A horrible suspicion set the lawyer's brain on fire. Had Aubrey been watching him through the chink in the door? But that could hardly be. Another pang shot through his heart. A strong shudder racked his body. He clutched at the table, missed it, and fell to the floor. Aubrey Leclair smiled at him.

"Aubrey!"

It was the lawyer who spoke. His whole body was convulsed from the poison.

"Yes, Aubrey?"

The apothecary smiled again.

"Aubrey! Did you—did you change the glasses?"

The smile vanished from the lips of Aubrey the apothecary as he leaned over his dying enemy. His brows were knit in anger, and hate sat on his face like a dark cloud.

"Yes, Aubrey, I changed the glasses."

The apothecary's voice thrilled with triumph.

"You are caught in your own death-trap," he continued. "I would not drink your wine, for I knew you had poisoned it. While you were in the inner office I changed glasses. I not only gave you the glass you intended for me, but I poisoned your wine myself, to make sure. I took no chances."

Now it was Aubrey the lawyer who smiled, as he lay in convulsions on the floor.

"Then we shall meet again," he said weakly. "Au revoir, Aubrey, but not good-bye. Au revoir! Au rev—"

He made a final attempt to rise, but suddenly pitched forward on his face. His body slowly stiffened.

Aubrey Leclair did not see him die, for he had suddenly gone blind. He groped toward the table. His foot caught on the head of Aubrey Charles. With a half-smothered cry he fell across the body of the lawyer, and a moment later he was dead.

THE WHITE QUEEN

Oriental Stories, October/November 1930

It was Bishop Fergus who suggested that his daughter's future should be staked on the hazard of a chess game.

"But that is gambling!" cried Fenworth, appalled. "Why not let Constance decide the matter herself? She is the one most vitally concerned."

Bishop Fergus looked over the side of Granby's yacht and stared meditatively into the Persian Gulf. His massive, nobly molded face and chiseled forehead, aureoled with an ample crop of snowy hair, looked like the carved bust of a Roman senator. Apparently he was lost in contemplation of the sand riffles on the bar that held the yacht fast a hundred yards from the Arabian shore, but in reality he was deep in thought. He twirled his spectacles absently by the black ribbon that held them. With his left hand he rubbed his smoothly shaven chin.

Suddenly he whirled around and faced his daughter, who was gazing at him with a world of entreaty in her eyes. He glanced from her to Fenworth, back to the girl, and looked at Fenworth again.

"Constance is only nineteen," he said. "She can not possibly know her own mind, and she is altogether too young to marry."

"But Father——" Constance interrupted.

The bishop raised his hand and continued hastily:

"No, no, do not break in. Hear me out, for, after all, I am your father and whatever I do will be with your best interests in mind.—Fenworth, you loved Constance before ever you came on board. If I had known that before we left San Francisco, then you never would have started. When old Granby placed his yacht at my disposal for a trip to the Holy Land, and you asked to go as my secretary, you kept to yourself your love for Constance. That was dishonest. Oh yes it was, Fenworth! You knew I never would take you along if I had suspected such a thing. But we had not been on the ocean two hours before I saw how matters stood.

"I like you, Fenworth, in every capacity except that of son-in-law. Now that you have come to me and asked for my consent, I could refuse to give it, but I must have your acquiescence. I must not be opposed in this matter. That is why I am putting it to the test of a game of chess. You have boasted of your prowess. I, too, am a chess-player, although I have not touched a piece in twenty years. There is a chessboard in Granby's cabin. I will play you one game. If you lose, you must break off this foolish love affair at once."

"And if I win?" Fenworth faltered, disquieted.

The bishop shrugged his shoulders impatiently.

"If you win I shall cease to oppose you, but I can't promise to co-operate."

Fenworth scanned the bishop's face, without answering. The bishop averted his eyes, and continued nervously twirling his glasses.

"Come, come," he said at last. "Will you play?"

"But that is gambling," Fenworth repeated again. "You are a bishop."

"Chess is never gambling, no matter what is at stake," the bishop affirmed. "Chance plays no part in it, for it is purely a game of skill. You are a good player, are you not?"

Fenworth did not reply, but continued to stare into the bishop's face.

"Much better than the average, I take it," the bishop continued, with a suggestion of sarcasm in his voice. "A really fine player, perhaps?"

"Father!" Constance admonished him.

The asperity in his voice amazed and wounded her.

"An uncommonly brilliant player, I believe?" the bishop continued, not heeding his daughter's interruption.

"Yes, sir," Fenworth answered, nettled. "I think I may say so without boasting, if past achievements prove anything. I am the best in the chess club. I won the intercity trophy two years running."

"Very good, then," Bishop Fergus continued, smiling blandly and rubbing his hands together rather gleefully. "In that case, it would seem that I am taking all the risks, and you none. Bring up the board, my boy. You will find it behind the book-shelf in Granby's cabin, and the chessmen are in the table drawer."

His face beamed as he saw Fenworth disappear. Not for weeks had he seemed so happy.

"Father, you mustn't," Constance pleaded.

"Constance, please do not oppose me," he ordered.

A huge red, green and yellow umbrella was put into place on the deck, and Fenworth sat down in its shade with Bishop Fergus to play for the bishop's daughter. The sky-blue water lapped gently against the sides of the yacht, and the hot sun rained its rays upon the yellow sand of the desert, a scant hundred yards distant. Not a sound broke the stillness, except the droning of the desert flies, for the boat's machinery was stopped.

The position of the stranded yacht had been wirelessed, and help was on the way from Muscat. To the two lovers the delay caused by this side trip up the Persian Gulf had meant merely another week of paradise, but now the bishop had ended it all by proposing his absurd chess game.

Constance watched the movements of the little carved ivory horses and bishops and foot-soldiers with vast interest. She did not understand the moves, but those sinister-looking warriors were fighting out her destiny. A dark red knight on horseback tore through Fenworth's line of pawns and demolished two white foot-soldiers and a saintly-looking white bishop with flowing beard before it was captured and removed from the board. The dark knight looked so evil and terrible and it moved about the board in such an erratic and apparently illogical way that Constance conceived a terror of it. She stared at the two pieces as they stood side by side on the table, after they were removed, the saintly white bishop with a smile on its face and the dark horseman glowering.

She turned from the discarded pieces to look again at the game as the other dark knight was laid low in exchange for one of Fenworth's white knights. Constance felt somehow happier, knowing that the two evil-looking horsemen were removed from the board. Anxiously she studied Fenworth's face. He seemed worried. In truth, the game was going not at all to his liking. Bishop Fergus had forced a terrific attack upon his queen, which could not be rescued without the absolute sacrifice of a piece.

Fenworth sank dispiritedly lower and lower in his chair, desperately pondering his next move. Suddenly his hand trembled and he shot at Constance a glance of hope. He sat up straight in his chair. His heart beat so loudly that he feared the bishop must hear it. He tried to maintain his calm, but only the bishop's preoccupation with the game prevented him from detecting the new hope and anxiety in Fenworth's face.

After carefully studying the board before him, Fenworth deliberately abandoned the white queen to capture and moved his remaining white knight into position for an attack upon his opponent's king. If Bishop Fergus should take Fenworth's queen instead of building up a defense for the king, then Fenworth would win the game within four moves.

Would the bishop see his danger? He considered his next move for what to Fenworth was an interminable time, poising his hand over the white queen as if about to capture it. Fenworth restrained his jubilation, and the bishop withdrew his hand and pondered again. Fenworth raised his eyes from the board and looked across the yellow sand of the desert, seeking even a stunted tree on which to rest his gaze. Only a cloud of dust, probably a mile away. He turned again to the board.

Would the bishop never move? His finely carved head was still bent over the game as he studied the positions of the pieces, holding the edge of his spectacles against his lips. He saw danger threatening him in Fenworth's move, but he did not see the inevitable checkmate that would defeat him if he captured his opponent's queen.

Both players were so intent on their game that they did not hear a smothered exclamation from Constance, who was looking out over the desert, watching the cloud of dust draw rapidly nearer. The bishop's fingers closed over the white queen and lifted the piece from the board.

"Checkmate!" Fenworth shouted jubilantly.

"Checkmate?" the bishop echoed incredulously.

"In four moves!" Fenworth explained joyously. "You

should have perfected your defense. But now——"

His sentence remained unfinished, for Constance cried out again, sharply. Fenworth sensed alarm in her tones, and he sprang to her side, overturning the board and spilling the chessmen. The girl's eyes were fixed upon the desert.

Fenworth glanced across the ribbon of shallow water that separated the grounded yacht from the shore. A troop of Arabian horsemen was spurring directly toward him. They were already within a few hundred yards of the water's edge, and riding full tilt for the yacht. The sand flew out in clouds behind them. The little stretch of desert that intervened narrowed rapidly and disappeared under a rush of flying feet and the splashing of horses' hoofs into the warm water of the Persian Gulf.

The troop rode across the shallow water of the sand bar, and in another moment were beside the yacht. They uttered not a sound, these silent men of the desert, but stood on the backs of their steeds and came up the side of the yacht hand over hand, leaving the horses champing in the water.

One of the Arabs seized Constance, who struggled and cried out. Fenworth, recovering from the amazement that had paralyzed him, lifted a camp-stool. Before he could swing it, another Arab deftly twisted his arm. The stool fell to the deck, and Fenworth was quickly thrown and trussed. The crew of the yacht was overpowered with ease. The skipper had not even the opportunity to seize his revolver. The Bedouins bound them each and every one, and passed them over the side of the yacht to the men below like sacks of flour.

Speechlessly, as they had come, the Bedouins rode away across the desert with their captives. The sun poured down

mercilessly, and the cruel thongs cut into the flesh. The bishop suffered perhaps worse than the others, but he had no thought of complaint for himself. He cried out several times to Constance, who was carried by a handsome young Arab with short, silky black beard and prominent forehead, and black eyes that shone brilliantly, like polished ebony. He held her before him on the shoulders of his black mare, and occasionally he lifted her in his strong arms and swung her around so that she could be more comfortable.

The bishop was carried by an old, cruel-looking Arab whose beard was streaked with gray, and who was absolutely indifferent to the comfort of his captive. Fenworth swung precariously across the neck of a swift roan, in front of a tall, strong Bedouin whose mask-like face gave no hint of what thoughts might lie behind it. Before long he suffered acute pain from his uncomfortable and cramped position. The pitiless heat made him dizzy as they rode into the face of the westering sun.

As they faced more and more that blazing disk, Constance's captor pulled the hood of his burnoose down over his forehead to keep out the sun, and turned the girl more and more toward him to shield her from the glare. Thus the two found themselves gazing into each other's eyes. Frank admiration gleamed in the Bedouin's lustrous black eyes, and he held her very firmly and gently, as the girl duly observed in spite of her fright.

The ground became more uneven, and was cut up by wadies. The troop crossed the dry beds of several, and Fenworth involuntarily cried out at the rough jolting as the horses loped down and up again. But the Bedouin who held Constance lifted her tenderly in his arms as they went across the wadies, and protected her from the jolting.

At length, as the sun was touching the rim of the desert, the troop, at a sharp command from the Arab who held Constance, turned north up a wady, where the going was easier than across the open desert. They followed the wady for perhaps half an hour, then turned westward again at another command and rode slowly up a long hill. The barking of dogs and the cries of children were borne to the ears of the prisoners. As they reached the summit, Constance's captor turned her around so that she could look down.

She gasped in astonishment. Spread out before her in the dusk was no temporary tent-village of nomads, but permanent buildings, waving palms, and a great pool of water. They had been brought to an oasis in the most inhospitable part of the Arabian desert, and a welcome sight it was to the travel-worn captives.

The Bedouins broke their silence for the first time that

day, and began to talk excitedly among themselves. They carefully picked their way among a band of sheep, then broke into a gallop and charged down into the oasis.

A mob of dirty children and barking dogs immediately surrounded them, and several youths ran over to the arriving horsemen. A huge black slave, wearing the burnoose of the Arabs, stood motionless before the doorway of the most pretentious of the buildings, fixing his gaze with utmost interest upon the strangers.

To Constance, when her bonds were removed and she was placed upon her feet, they seemed to have arrived in some storied village out of the *Arabian Nights*. A large central building in Moorish style, made out of colored clays, slender beams and curiously cut stone, stood immediately in front of them. Radiating from this were galleries, like the cloister of a monastery. Behind them were the low mud dwellings of the Arabs, ornamented, like the central building, with colored clays and carved wood. A large pool, bordered with date palms, lay to their right, and to this pool the whinnying horses were allowed to stray.

The prisoners were led at once through the portal of the main building, past the stolid black slave, and conducted into a central court. There they were grouped around a fountain, which flowed slowly through the court. Its waters were carried away to the pool through a stone gutter.

The young man who had carried Constance left them standing by the fountain while he went through an arched doorway into an inner room. He returned almost immediately with a gray-bearded man, whose entrance the other Bedouins acknowledged by profound bows. He was clad in spotless white, and wore about his neck a sparkling necklace from which depended a large black pearl. The deference paid him by the others, the air of mastery with which he approached the prisoners, the whiteness of his garments, all marked him as one who possessed authority. His vivid black eyes looked out upon the world through deep wrinkles, and his expression was the incarnation of curiosity and eagerness. With cautious dread Constance studied his face, bronzed and chiseled by the winds of the desert. He might be either good or bad, for all that she could read in his countenance. Certain it is that his face at the moment looked kindly rather than hostile.

The Arab approached the bishop.

"English?" he asked.

"No. We are Americans," the bishop replied.

"But you know how to speak English?"

"Yes," said the bishop.

"That is good," the Arab answered, a million wrinkles carving his face as he smiled. "You are no longer prisoners, for you were also our allies. I was with Lawrence in the war against the Ottomans. I am the Sheik Ferhan ibn Hedeb, and you are my guests. Smeyr!" he called, raising his voice and clapping his hands thrice.

The black slave who had stood before the entrance came quickly in and prostrated himself before his master in a profound salaam. Sheik Ferhan gave a few crisp orders in Arabic, and Smeyr retreated backward through the door.

"Smeyr will have the women place dwellings in order for you," said the sheik. "He will be the slave of the lady during your visit. I have place for several of you in the palace, and the rest must stay in the dwellings."

Sheik Ferhan glanced around with the pride of possession.

"Now I would know the names of my eminent guests," he continued, "and chiefly the name of this lady, who is a dream of beauty."

He bowed low, and Constance flushed.

"This is my daughter Constance," the bishop said. "I am Bishop Fergus of San Francisco, and this is Fenworth, the young man who is one day to be the husband of my daughter."

Fenworth gave Constance a quick look, and the flush on her cheek became deeper. Sheik Ferhan's appraising glance covered Fenworth from the soles of his feet to the crown of his head.

"Smeyr!" he cried, as the black returned.

He gave further commands, and the slave extended his hands and stood expectantly to one side.

"Smeyr will lead your people to their dwellings, Bishop," the sheik explained. "You and your beautiful daughter will remain here, with your friend. In thirty minutes all will return and take lebben. You are very tired. You will rest here—three, five, seven days, perhaps. Then you will be taken back to your ship. I am most unhappy that my men caused trouble to you, but most happy that you are here. I will show you the hospitality of Bedouins, like nothing else in the world. Do you like lebben?"

"Lebben?" the bishop repeated. "I do not know the word."

"Our goat's milk, soured and fermented. Very good, very strong, very stimulating. But there will also be dates, and my women will prepare sweet goat's milk for the lady. I am told that your women always drink their milk unsoured."

Sheik Ferhan himself conducted the bishop, Constance and Fenworth to their rooms. Smeyr returned shortly, and carried to Constance a huge basin of water. He discreetly withdrew, and knocked on the post of her doorway when he thought a sufficient time had elapsed for her to prepare her toilet. She handed the basin back to him through the curtains that served as door, and the black then carried it to the bishop, and afterward to Fenworth, without changing the water.

A few minutes later Sheik Ferhan called to his guests, and they came out into the court, where they were joined shortly by the remaining members of the bishop's party. Seating Constance on his right and her father on his left, the sheik sat cross-legged on the floor. A bowl of soured milk was placed before each of the guests, and the sheik's women passed around salvers piled high with golden dates. Constance drank a long draft of goat's milk. Sheik Ferhan did not partake, aside from taking a few dates, explaining that he had eaten his daily meal some hours before.

"But in my country we eat three times a day!" Constance exclaimed.

"Three times!" Sheik Ferhan echoed. "Then why do you not become fat and ugly, like the Ottoman women? But no, you are thin and graceful, like a fox. I think you eat very little at each sitting."

He looked well pleased with himself for his compliments. Constance dimpled, and Fenworth looked grave.

After the meal, Sheik Ferhan clapped his hands four times, and the Arabs who had captured the bishop's party came into the court. They bowed low, and then came over to the sheik, bowing once again. The tall, handsome Bedouin who had carried Constance was introduced to her as Zadd. He bowed low before her, and touched her hand with his fingers, pronouncing the name "Constance" very carefully. He was presented to each of the party, and then, bowing low again before the sheik, he and his companions departed.

"Zadd wants the lady to know his great sorrow at your discomfort," Sheik Ferhan explained. "We are all sorry to annoy you, but happy, very, very happy, to have you with us. Every house is open to you. Ask for what you wish, and it shall be yours. If you have coins about you, my people will be glad to have some. But you must offer them when you enter their houses. Then they are gifts. No Bedouin will take pay for hospitality, but they like coins as gifts. They are very proud, my Bedouins. Two centuries on the oasis have not made fellahs of us. But now you are very tired. You will want sleep. Tomorrow will be time to see my people and my good oasis. Peace to you!"

Bowing deeply, he withdrew. Smeyr conducted the crew of the yacht to their dwellings, and the bishop, Constance and Fenworth went to their rooms.

Constance lay wide-eyed on the woolen mattress in her room, thinking over the exciting events of the day. She had never met anyone quite so courtly as the old sheik, who had rescued her and her party from the hands of his tribesmen. She thought of the tales of Harun-al-Rashid, and drifted insensibly into slumber. Sheik Ferhan, Harun-al-Rashid and the handsome Zadd were inextricably mixed in her dreams.

Bishop Fergus, his mind relieved by the benevolent protection of the sheik, soon dropped to sleep, despite the soreness of his body after the long ride across the desert.

Fenworth, alone of all the party from the yacht, did not

sleep. He had seen the look of admiration on Zadd's patrician face while crossing the sands, and although he was too much preoccupied with his own discomfort and danger to think much about it then, it troubled him now. But what the attitude of Sheik Ferhan might be troubled Fenworth even more. The young American had watched the sheik closely during the meal, and in his face he read shrewdness and crafty cunning. To Fenworth it was obvious that Sheik Ferhan desired Constance. A look of annoyance had darkly wrinkled the sheik's face when the bishop told him that Fenworth was to marry Constance. The look disappeared almost as soon as it was born, but Fenworth had seen it, and it made him tremble.

Another man slept but little that night, had Fenworth but known it. That man was Zadd, for he, too, had looked upon Constance, and he, too, had seen the look of desire in the eyes of Sheik Ferhan. The sheik had promised protection to the party, and henceforth the Americans were no longer prisoners, but guests, and every member of the tribe was bound by the laws of Bedouin hospitality to treat them as friends. But for some reason that he could not explain, some imperceptible insincerity in Sheik Ferhan's manner, or perhaps only an impalpable and meaningless shadow of fear, Zadd was troubled.

Constance awoke early, and was about to arise when one of the sheik's women came into the room, bearing a basin of water and a coarse linen towel. Her ablutions finished, Constance entered the court. Fenworth was there before her, pacing stiffly back and forth, keeping watch on her door. As the curtain was pushed aside he came forward eagerly and greeted her with a betrothal kiss, the first he had been able to give her since he won her at chess the day before. The bishop joined them a few minutes later, walking slowly, sore and weary from his ride across the desert.

"Happy morning!"

The three turned quickly as Sheik Ferhan entered the court. He was smiling broadly. Three women accompanied him, bearing milk, butter and dates for the breakfast. The sheik again declined food, but sat and talked with his guests while they ate.

"I am a Bedouin," he said. "One meal a day is enough. If I ate more I might become fat, and that would be ugly. I have great wish to show our oasis to you, and we shall have horses racing. And you must meet my wife. I have but one, although the great Prophet (on whom be peace!) allows four to every man who, like myself, can give the necessaries of life to so many."

He smiled his broad smile, his little black eyes twinkling and little wrinkles radiating good-humoredly from the corners.

"Come, my friends," he said, smiling again, and stroking his grizzled beard, "I will show to you the hareem."

He offered Constance his arm, with all the courtly grace of a Solomon greeting Sheba's queen. Constance laughed delightedly and went with him through the curtains into the secret recesses of the dwelling. Her father followed with Fenworth. A tall woman, arrayed in spotless white, without a veil, waited in the harem, attended by two women slaves. She evidently expected the visit.

"My one and only wife, Adooba," said Sheik Ferhan, saluting her with a deferential bow.

He added a few words in Arabic. Adooba smiled, and bowed to the three guests in turn. She looked keenly at

Constance. Fenworth, watching her narrowly, saw distrust written on that desert-bronzed countenance.

Conversation was impossible; so, after an interchange of formalities through the sheik, they passed the baths of the hareem and went out into the open air, the sheik and Constance leading. Zadd and one other, who served as interpreter, awaited them, and the black Smeyr followed a few paces in the rear. Smeyr never left the party throughout the day.

Zadd's companion, in very bad English, introduced himself to Fenworth and the bishop as Faris, who served with General Townshend's army in the advance on Bagdad. While Sheik Ferhan explained everything to Constance, Faris tried to do the same for the bishop and Fenworth.

"I learned English very good," he explained. "I interpreter at English army. I interpret you oasis. Here big water pool—water tree, goat, sheep, horse, men. Here horse run for you this today. Ten, and ten more, with Zadd on black she-horse. You see, after dinner."

The party completed its tour by visiting the mud houses. The crew of the yacht had already struck up an acquaintance with the Arabs the evening before, through the medium of Faris, who had suggested that they would like gold coins as keepsakes, and was desolated to find that the Americans had no coins in their pockets when they were dragged from the yacht.

All of the Americans—Constance, Fenworth, the bishop, and the fourteen men of the crew—gathered in the sheik's courtyard for the noon meal. Zadd and Faris formed part of the party, and Adooba, who usually ate in the hareem, sat silently beside her lord as a special honor to the strangers. The sheik's women brought heaping trays of dates and bowls of milk, and a huge wooden platter containing the great fat tail of a sheep, surrounded by splintered masses of cooked mutton. Bones and meat were mangled together and boiled without seasoning. Lumps of butter and dough were ranged around the edge of the platter, and bits of liver surrounded the tail of the sheep.

The meal was far from appetizing, and there were no plates from which to eat it. The platter was first placed in front of Sheik Ferhan, who handed it on to Constance and instructed her how to eat from it. He passed a little dish of salt to her, and she dipped her fingers into the meat, salted it and tasted it. She did not like it, and turned her attention to the milk and dates, while the sheik passed the platter to Adooba. Then he ate from the platter himself, and it was passed in turn to the bishop, Fenworth, and the members of the crew. There was much of the strange food left when it reached Zadd and Faris, and the sheep's tail had not been touched, but they fell upon it like hungry wolves, and passed the scraps to Smeyr.

Bowls of water from the fountain were then passed among the guests, and the party arose and proceeded to the smooth plain at the west of the pool, where the races were to be run.

Twenty young Arabs rode in the first race, which Zadd easily won on a speedy little black mare. Then came spear-throwing, foot-racing between the youths of the oasis, and pitching of quoits. Sheik Ferhan explained the sports to Constance, and Fenworth chafed at the attentions he paid her, for the newly engaged young man had hardly had a word with his sweetheart all day. He found his opportunity to join her after the races, when the sheik dropped back to chat with the bishop.

"It's about time," Fenworth commented ill-naturedly, as he took the sheik's place at Constance's side. "I thought that old mage was going to stick to you forever. He must bore you frightfully.'

"On the contrary," Constance said, "I think he's clever. He is certainly terribly interesting. I believe I like him immensely."

"You're as bad as the White Queen in *Through the Looking-Glass*, who believed six impossible things before breakfast," Fenworth growled.

"Surly you aren't jealous of a nice old Arab sheik," Constance replied.

"Why," Sheik Ferhan was asking the bishop at the same moment, "why is your daughter going to marry that young man?"

"He is really very worthy," the bishop answered. "And besides, he won my daughter in a chess game. They are to be married on our return to San Francisco."

"What a pity!" Sheik Ferhan replied, shaking his head and stroking his grizzled beard. "What a pity!" he repeated, with a look of great shrewdness in his eyes. "So he won your daughter in a chess game."

For a minute he was deep in thought. A merry laugh from Constance broke up his revery, and he raised his head almost fiercely.

"Fenworth!" he spoke out sharply, in a tone of command.

Fenworth looked up. Sheik Ferhan rose and came toward him. His eyes were twinkling, and the little wrinkles at their corners writhed in mirthful exultation.

"You are a player of chess," he said, with a suggestion of contempt in his voice. "Tomorrow you will display your ability. You will play with me a game, and the chessmen will be living men and women, and the pieces will walk across a giant checkerboard marked out on the plain. You and I will direct them from a platform built like a tower at one end of the field. The beautiful Constance will be the white queen, and Adooba will be the dark queen. It is fitting so, for Adooba's face has been darkened by the sun, but the face of the American girl is white like milk. You have seventeen persons in your party from the ship. You will play, and the other sixteen will be pieces in our game. The castles will ride on camels, and the knights will ride on mares, that we may know them as we overlook the checkerboard from our tower. The bishops will be robed in long white burnooses, and the pawns will walk on foot. Thus will there be a game that will amuse us for half a day."

"But not for a stake," Fenworth interposed. "I won Constance once in a game, and I don't want to stake my fortune again in that way."

Sheik Ferhan's face became terrible, but the cloud passed on the instant and his face wrinkled again in a smile.

"If I wished to have that beautiful girl in my harem," he said, "I would ask her, and not come to you. A woman loves, or she does not love, and the hazard of a game can not change it. Smeyr!"

He brought his palms together sharply, and Smeyr was before him almost immediately. The sheik gave him orders in Arabic, and he withdrew at once.

"Over there will be the platform," said Sheik Ferhan. "Here will be the field. We will mark the dark squares by rugs and cloths, and the sandy ground will be the white squares. But you would now eat dates and milk. I find the Americans do not like lebben. But dates and milk there are for all. We will now withdraw to the palace that the Americans may eat."

The repast over, Sheik Ferhan suggested to Constance that they go out by the pool and watch the moon.

"They tell me," he said, "that at Mecca the moon looks just the same as it does here. Do you see the moon in San Francisco?"

As they came into the open and saw the moon silvering the desert, Constance tugged at Sheik Ferhan's sleeve.

"Oh, beautiful!" she exclaimed. "I have seen the moon just as it is now, as I looked across the water from the ocean beach, by the Cliff House in San Francisco, and I have watched it sink lower and lower until it was drowned by the swell of the Pacific Ocean."

"Then the moon must shine everywhere," Sheik Ferhan said, measuring his words. "I do not understand. It is here, and it is there at the same time. Mecca lies across the desert, hundreds of miles south, almost within sight of the other sea, on the other side of the land. And Aleppo is far away, north of the sunset, in the Ottoman country, yet the same moon shines there. And London and San Francisco are at the ends of the world, farther even than Aleppo, and they all have the same moon. My poor brain can not understand it."

Constance laughed. Her mirth seemed to please the sheik, for the crow's-feet around his eyes wrinkled even more than usual, and he beamed ecstatically.

"But you will teach me many things, about the moon, and the ocean, and your country, and I will learn from you each day, oh palm-like stranger from across the water."

Constance looked at him wide-eyed.

"But I am to return!" she exclaimed. "You don't mean—you can't mean you will hold me here!"

"Your beauty is like the palms waving in the moonlight, after a weary ride across the sands," said Sheik Ferhan. "It tells of sweet repose and whispers of cooling waters and fragrant flowers. I am like a wanderer in the desert. I have been lost in the sands, and you are the oasis that tells me I have found my rest. You are not fat and ugly like the Ottoman women, nor dark like my own race. Listen, daughter of strangers. My wife Adooba is very sweet, but you are far sweeter than she. The great Prophet had four wives, which Allah allowed to him. I have but one. You will rule my harem, and the black slave-girls will serve you, and you will be my second and favorite wife."

Constance kept her eyes fixed on Sheik Ferhan during this speech. He hung his head, as abashed as a schoolboy declaring his love. His crafty glance sought Constance's face and shifted again to the ground.

"The great game of chess on the plain tomorrow will celebrate our wedding," he added, thoughtfully.

Then his arm encircled her and drew her to him, and his eyes sought her face. Constance struggled and pushed him away. He released her and gazed fiercely into her terrified eyes, reading there her horror and fright.

"You prefer the weak young man from San Francisco?"

Constance nodded.

The sheik's tone became hard.

"Very well, then. The Sheik Ferhan is refused. The weak young man from across the water is winner. Then let him earn his prize. Let him look well to his game, as we move our human chessmen across the checkerboard tomorrow."

He meditated a minute. His face became tender.

"Let us go inside," he said. "Your weak young man with the white face will be impatient."

He bowed low and motioned to her to precede him.

An excited whispering caused her to turn her head. Two white figures were moving by the date trees at the pool's edge. She wondered if they had overheard Sheik Ferhan's declaration. The sheik saw them, too, but made no sign. The moon shone upon their faces, and Constance thought she recognized them as they withdrew into the inky shadow of the palms. One was Faris, the interpreter. The other was Zadd.

The shouting of children, the barking of dogs, the chanting of a Bedouin and the hum of voices woke Constance at daybreak. She arose and dressed, and found Fenworth and her father already pacing the court. She ran to her father and threw her arms about his neck. Fenworth stood by, vaguely troubled, and as Constance told of Sheik Ferhan's proposal the young man clenched his fists in impotent anger.

Two Arab women entered the court with trays of dates and figs, and pitchers of goat's milk. A minute later Sheik Ferhan joined the party and bade them good morning. He seated himself, smiling craftily, but did not partake of the food, as it was far from mealtime for him.

"The workmen are preparing the field," he said. "It will be ready very soon, and we shall have rare sport. With you directing, there will be just enough persons in your party to be pieces and pawns on your side. The fair Constance and the dark Adooba will be our queens. We will have a pretty game, very good to look at."

He clapped his hands, and Zadd and Faris came to his

side. Shortly thereafter Adooba joined the group, and they proceeded toward the field, Sheik Ferhan walking with his wife, while Constance walked between her father and Fenworth. Zadd and Faris brought up the rear.

Constance clapped her hands in pleasurable excitement at the sight that greeted her. A huge checkerboard was mapped out on the plain. Rugs formed the dark squares, and gleaming sand the white squares. At the outer edge, toward the desert, and between the opposing groups, was built a platform ten feet high, from which Sheik Ferhan and Fenworth were to direct their human chessmen. Opposite, in the blacker sand of the oasis, the sheik's workmen had sunk a hollow pit, which was filled with water. Beside this stood Smeyr, clad only in a snowy white girdle, his giant black limbs and body shining in the sun. At a signal from Sheik Ferhan he lifted high a huge bowl.

"This is the water clock, by which our moves will be timed," Sheik Ferhan explained.

He spoke to Smeyr, and the black cast the bowl down upon the pool. It began to fill with water, which forced its way through a hole in the bottom. The bowl settled lower and lower.

"It takes ten minutes for the water to fill the bowl so that it will sink," Sheik Ferhan explained. "As soon as you have made your first move, Fenworth, Smeyr will let the bowl fall upon the water and I will have ten minutes to make my move. If I have not moved before the bowl sinks, Smeyr will strike this brazen gong to show me that my time is used up and I must make my move at once. Whenever a piece is ordered moved, then Smeyr will empty the bowl and let it fall again upon the water, and the other player will have ten minutes to think out his next move, if he wishes to take that long. But let us begin."

He gave a few sharp commands to Zadd and Faris, and soon the human pieces were in motion toward the checkerboard. Camels stood at the board's four corners, awaiting their riders. Next these, on the north and south edges of the mammoth board, were hobbled mares for the knights to ride—white mares for Fenworth's side, black mares for Sheik Ferhan. Bishop Fergus and the skipper of the yacht, in long white burnooses, took their positions on the squares next to the mares, to be the white bishops in this strange tourney. On Sheik Ferhan's side two patriarchal Bedouins with gray beards were the bishops.

The sheik himself escorted Adooba to the queen's square, and Constance, mistaking her place, walked to the white king's square, from which Fenworth laughingly shifted her to the queen's square adjoining. The pompous cook from the yacht, with an improvised crown on his head, stepped to the king's place. In front of each of the opposing lines of pieces, after much laughter and confusion, were at length ranged the pawns—the eight remaining members of the yacht's crew on Fenworth's side, and eight young Arabs on Sheik Ferhan's side.

Then the sheik and Fenworth, accompanied by Zadd and Faris, made their way to the platform. A small checkerboard was placed between the two players on a little table, with ivory and ebony chessmen, that they might direct the human pieces by their mimic counterparts. Zadd and Faris stood on the platform with folded arms as Sheik Ferhan and Fenworth took their seats.

Then Sheik Ferhan spoke. His voice was calm and even, and bore no trace of the passion that guided his words. Fenworth, watching him intently, read his feelings only in the narrowing of his eyes. Zadd, uncomprehending, stood impassive, but Faris, the interpreter, started, and on his face were dismay and consternation.

"Young man with the weak face," said Sheik Ferhan, softly, "last night I offered the American girl the honor of ruling my harem as my second and favorite wife. She refused. You, and she, and all of you, are my guests, by my own act, although my men hoped to hold you for ransom, when they captured you. I could have kept you as prisoners, but I did not. But the American girl has hurt me—here!"

With a theatrical gesture, he struck his clenched fist upon his heart.

"However," he continued, quickly recovering his tranquillity, "I shall not force her into my hareem. But I can not forget the hurt. I am a Bedouin, and therefore proud. Young man with the weak face, if you love this girl you must fight for her. You must prove your right to her in this chess game. Listen well to me, and hear my offer.

"If you lose, then you, and she, and all of you, will be sent into slavery among the lost oases. Your Europeans' maps do not show them, and your travelers have never visited them. Your consuls and your soldiers can never find you. You will disappear, and be heard of no more. And you will be separated from the American girl. She has refused the honor of becoming my wife. I accept this fate, but she will grace the hareem of some sheik in the lost oases.

"But if you win, then you, and those of your people who are not captured in our friendly game of chess, will be sent back to your ship, with all the gifts my little wealth can provide. If you still keep your white queen uncaptured, then you can take her with you, But if she, or her father, or any other of your people are removed from this great checkerboard, then they will be sent as slaves to the lost oases, and the rest of you will return to your ship. Do you understand?"

Fenworth set his lips tightly together. An unwonted pallor blenched his cheeks. He looked steadily into Sheik Ferhan's eyes, and the old man's gaze fell before the American's stare.

"Come, young man with the weak face." said Sheik Ferhan, "I will be fair. I tell you that the American girl will be sold into a hareem if you lose her in this game, but I offer you Adooba if you remove her from the checkerboard in our game of chess. What is fair to me is fair to you. Win the game and capture the dark queen, then you may take Adooba away to your ship. And if I capture the white queen, then you lose the American girl. I warn you that I am an excellent player. Many nights I played with the English officers and beat them badly. Let us begin."

Zadd raised his hand at the sheik's command, and Smeyr struck the gong. A brazen note rolled over the plain. The chess game had begun.

Fenworth carefully advanced the pawn in front of the dignified cook from the yacht, who stood in haughty majesty, with his mimic crown, for all the world like a real king standing before his throne. The gong sounded again, and Sheik Ferhan ordered his own king's pawn into the center of the board. Zadd shouted his orders in Arabic, and the black, who had cast down the water clock upon the pool, picked up the bowl and emptied it. Sheik Ferhan's move was duplicated on the field, and Smeyr cast the empty bowl upon the pool.

That part of the Arab population not engaged in the

game crowded around the mammoth checkerboard and watched in fascinated but uncomprehending interest the progress of the play. Women and children elbowed and jostled one another as Zadd and Faris ran among the living figures of the game directing their movements according to the moves made by Fenworth and Sheik Ferhan with the carved ivory and ebony pieces on the platform.

Again and again Smeyr struck the brazen gong, emptied the bowl, and cast it down again upon the pool. Cautiously the two players maneuvered their black and white pieces, and Zadd and Faris duplicated the movements on the field, sometimes shouting out the directions, and sometimes leaving the platform and going out among the human pieces. The women laughed as the hobbled mares lumbered over the squares, bearing the knights on their backs, and the children clapped their hands in gleeful excitement. But Fenworth sat silently, with mouth tightly compressed and eyes glued to the board in front of him, only raising his glance from time to time to make certain that Faris had properly repeated his move among the human chessmen on the plain. He castled, and a camel lumbered to its feet under Faris's blows. The children shouted as the ungainly beast, rocking from side to side, moved to the spot just vacated by Bishop Fergus, who had been shifted to the center of the board.

Then Sheik Ferhan moved out Adooba, using her to launch an attack against Fenworth's queen. Fenworth gazed fixedly at the position in front of him, as if to verify the danger in which the white queen stood, then shot a quick glance toward Constance. She blew a kiss to him and smiled radiantly, ignorant of the danger that enveloped her. Fenworth fixed his attention again upon the board, and blocked the sheik's move. Faris descended from the platform and duplicated the move upon the plain.

Sheik Ferhan darted one fierce glance at Fenworth, and set himself to the task of capturing the white queen and removing Constance from the field. He forced an exchange of knights, and the children shouted again as the hobbles were removed from the mares' legs and the riders dismounted.

The benignant smile faded from Bishop Fergus' face and he muttered an angry exclamation, for two Arabs from the sheik's household set upon the sailor who had been riding the mare as Fenworth's queen's knight, and bound him and laid him down upon the plain a prisoner. A murmur ran through the crew of the yacht, and the faces of the rest of the concourse expressed genuine surprize. Zadd stood for a moment stock-still, as if unable to trust his eyes. He expostulated with the two Arabs, but their explanation seemed to satisfy him, and he strode back to the platform. Smeyr struck the gong again and cast down the bowl upon the pool, and the play was resumed.

Now the two antagonists settled down to a terrific duel. Fenworth used the full ten minutes allotted to him for each play, but Sheik Ferhan made his decisions rapidly, moving the ebony pieces on the board almost as soon as Fenworth's moves were completed, and sending Zadd post-haste to carry out the maneuver on the field. Two of Fenworth's pawns were exchanged and set bound beside the sailor, and Zadd, still uncomprehending, remonstrated with the sheik. But Ferhan spoke sharply to him, and he descended from the platform to carry out the instructions of his chief.

The game was turning slowly in the sheik's favor, and Fenworth, trying desperately to save Constance, found himself open to a strong attack upon his king, an attack that seemed certain to win the game for Sheik Ferhan. But the Arab's reckless attack upon Constance had overreached itself. It exposed the sheik to the loss of a piece, and with it the game, for the players were too evenly matched for Sheik Ferhan to expect victory if Fenworth had the absolute advantage of a piece. To force the exchange and gain the piece, however, Fenworth would have to give up Constance in exchange for the Arab's queen.

Bishop Fergus saw the desperate plight of Fenworth's game, and realized Sheik Ferhan's treachery. The attack upon the white queen made him fear that the sheik planned to take Constance into his harem if he captured her in the play. He saw Constance's danger and knew that he was the buffer that must be interposed and exchanged to prevent an interchange of queens. He thrust two fingers into his mouth and whistled shrilly to attract Fenworth's attention.

Fenworth was conscious of a vast irritation. This was *his* game, not the bishop's. In that moment he hated the bishop for distracting his attention from the pieces before him. Had he not proved himself the better player by winning Constance from him? Why, then, did the bishop not keep out of it?

If he protected Constance by interposing her father, then only the flimsiest chance of winning remained to him, for the position against him was very strong. Slavery threatened all of them, and Sheik Ferhan had said that he and Constance would be sold to tribes quite far apart. He looked out over the field and saw that the water clock was slowly sinking. The minutes were creeping on, and beads of sweat stood out on Fenworth's forehead as he fought to decide his move within the time allotted to him.

If he should accept the exchange and surrender Constance to a temporary slavery, would not a rescue be possible? Most of the party would return to the yacht, and the American government would surely punish the sheik and find those whom he had sold into the lost oases. Had it not rescued an American citizen from the Moroccan bandit Raisuli? The skipper of the yacht was an Englishman, and the British government possessed great influence with the Bedouin tribes, because it had actively aided the Arabs in their struggle for independence. The British government could surely force the return of the prisoners. But if he protected Constance now and lost the game thereby, then all of them would be enslaved and no news of their fate would ever reach the outside world.

The cries of the Arab children had ceased. Everyone sensed some important decision to be made, and the throng hung upon the event with breathless interest, even though the spectators did not understand the maneuvers.

Hardly more than the rim of the bowl still showed above the surface of the pool. Fenworth scowled in silent rage. If the water clock would only give him more time to make up his mind! How could he think with that sinking bowl speeding away the seconds, and Bishop Fergus shouting at him?

He stared sullenly, unable to withdraw his eyes. The last few seconds seemed hours. What had that bowl to do with him, anyway? He experienced a strange anger at it.

And now the bowl swirled, and sank from sight. The huge black lifted his shining arm and struck a blow on the brazen gong. It seemed a full minute before the club in Smeyr's hand touched the gong and the harsh sound boomed discordantly through the air, but it was in reality only a small part of a second.

Fenworth's world seemed to fall away from him. He moved the ivory bishop to protect his queen, and Faris hastened to the field to duplicate the maneuver. He had made his decision and taken the fighting chance.

Sheik Ferhan without hesitation lifted the ivory bishop from the board, and sent Zadd to direct the removal of Bishop Fergus to the group of prisoners who sat, with arms bound behind them, near the water clock.

Now Faris, returning from directing Fenworth's move, encountered Zadd. He told him what Zadd already half suspected, and it made the tall Arab's handsome face become for the moment distorted with strong anger. Sheik Ferhan, from his place on the platform, called to him to hasten. Zadd gave Bishop Fergus over to the two Arabs from the sheik's household, and they tied his hands behind him. Smeyr cast down the bowl, and the game was on again.

Fenworth gnawed his thumb-nail and tried to see daylight through the gloom that enveloped him. On the board before him, as on the field beneath him, with carved or with human pieces, he saw defeat and slavery. The net drew tighter, and Fenworth struggled vainly, as the water clock again told off the seconds against him.

Zadd and Faris returned to the platform, and the handsome Bedouin spoke to Sheik Ferhan in low, measured tones. Fenworth, who knew no Arabic, nevertheless felt the restrained feeling that surged beneath Zadd's words. He saw the determined visage of the tall Arab, and the clenching and unclenching of his left hand as he spoke, and he saw the eyes of Sheik Ferhan narrow to mere slits.

Slowly the ancient sheik rose to his feet. As slowly as he had risen, he extended his right hand and grasped the hem of Zadd's burnoose. Speech poured from him in a flood, beginning low at first and swelling in angry volume as his voice rose higher and higher. Zadd closed the fingers of his powerful left hand around Sheik Ferhan's knuckles and wrenched his grasp from the burnoose. Then he deliberately pushed his chief to one side.

Raising his voice until it carried clearly across the giant checkerboard and rang out over the pool of the oasis, Zadd addressed the Arabs. He had uttered but a few words before Sheik Ferhan smote him upon the neck and tried to pull him from his perch.

Meantime Faris broke his silence and tried to explain to Fenworth what was happening.

"Zadd say Sheik Ferhan break Bedouin law. You no prisoner, you friend. Sheik must be friend to guest. Zadd say sheik break hospitality, make all you prisoner. He say Sheik Ferhan no more sheik."

Zadd broke the sheik's hold and sent the old man spinning into the board, knocking the pieces over. Sheik Ferhan crashed through the little table and fell from the platform to the ground, ten feet below, for there was no railing to break his momentum. He struck his head sharply against a corner post of the platform, and lay still on the ground.

The knights and castles and bishops and pawns came running swiftly across the sand to the base of the tower. Faris leapt the ten feet to the ground, and was first to reach his fallen chief. Zadd stood with folded arms, while Fenworth sat in his place amazed at the sudden passage of events.

Sheik Ferhan was dead. His neck had been broken as he fell head foremost from the platform. And now Zadd addressed the Arabs, vehemently at first, then more slowly and with more measured accents. What he said was gathered, bit by bit, from the hotchpotch of English that came from the willing but ineffectual lips of Faris.

"Your sheik has shamed you," said Zadd. "He made these strangers his guests, and by immemorial custom their persons were inviolate thereafter. He abused the sacred privilege of host and made prisoners of his guests. He proposed to sell them to the lost oases. He broke the law of hospitality, which is the worst crime a Bedouin can commit. Thereby he forfeited his right to the title of sheik. And now he lies dead. Peace be with him."

Silence greeted Zadd's solemn words, broken only by a stifled sob from Adooba. The dark queen of the oasis sincerely mourned her fallen lord. But on Zadd's heart also there lay a shadow, for his face was eloquent of gloom.

He conferred at once with the other leaders of the little tribe, and it was decided to send the Americans immediately to their yacht, in the half-day that remained before sunset. Zadd rode beside Constance, in silence, for how could these two converse, since neither knew the other's tongue? He threw over her shoulders a snowy white burnoose to protect her neck from the rain of heat rays, and he set a leisurely pace on his coal-black mare, so as not to weary the American girl.

He seldom looked at her, but Constance stole frequent glances into his finely formed face, with its strong nose and chin and short black beard. Fenworth rode immediately behind her, with an Arab escort, and the bishop rode third, beside Faris. Two by two, the party moved slowly across the desert.

The sun had set and the moon cast deep black shadows upon the yellow sand before they came within sight of old Granby's yacht. Still Zadd maintained the immobility of his countenance, and Constance gazed more and more often into his face. On the deck of the yacht several faces were seen, and a boat, with steam up, lay alongside. It was the relief boat from Muscat.

The Bedouins dismounted at a sign from Zadd, and Fenworth helped Constance to the ground. Faris again endeavored to convey his apologies for Sheik Ferhan's breach of hospitality. Then Zadd crisply ordered his followers to horse, and they rode away, each leading one of the horses that had brought the Americans back to the yacht.

Zadd was left with Constance. Diffidently he extended his hand in farewell greeting. She grasped it, and smiled into his face.

"Constance," he said, tenderly, and repeated the name carefully, several times: "Constance, Constance, Constance," as if to engrave it into his memory.

Her face betrayed the sadness of her heart as she scanned his features. He kept her hand in his and gazed fixedly into her eyes as the moon shone upon her upturned face. Then the girl kissed him on the mouth, in view of Fenworth and her father and the crew.

"Good-bye, Zadd, my sheik," she said, and her lips trembled.

Ashamed to let him see the moisture in her eyes, she turned away and strode to the water's edge, where she awaited passage to the yacht.

Zadd mounted the snow-white stallion that had brought her from the oasis. Leading his own coal-black mare, he loped back into the desert. Constance, looking from the deck of the yacht a few minutes later, saw silhouetted against the horizon two horses, and on one of them was a rider. They lingered for a little, and she tried to call to him.

"Good-bye, Zadd," she cried. "Good-bye!"

The silhouettes disappeared beyond the ridge, and Constance laid her head on Fenworth's shoulder and wept.

THE PICTURE OF JUDAS

Magic Carpet Magazine, April 1933

1

Buzzing like a swarm of bees, the group of choir singers walked rapidly through the narrow streets of Milan to see the restless Leonardo at work on his Cenacolo in the refectory of St. Mary of the Graces. The great Duomo, still uncompleted, towered behind them. The forest of white columns drew closer together as the choristers increased the distance, and the cathedral itself loomed vaster and more majestic as it receded. The chattering stopped as the singers entered the convent, and a twilight hush fell upon their lips. They crossed the portal into the refectory on tiptoe.

On the north wall of the long chamber was "The Last Supper," on which the painter had already spent three years. Two monks stood critically at one side, whispering together. In the back of the refectory, his eyes gazing into the picture from under shaggy eyebrows, sat Leonardo da Vinci.

He made a handsome figure, the young Leonardo, with his long, silky beard and commanding head. His aquiline nose was the embodiment of strength. The sensitive mouth, topped by narrow, long mustaches that tapered off into his beard, was firm and yet tender. Beetling brows overhung gray eyes that restlessly searched the world as if seeking what of truth or beauty lay there. The noble forehead, with its finely chiseled planes and its strength, dominated his splendid figure and gave to his appearance a commanding majesty that instantly challenged attention. His long, wavy locks were covered by a soft, black velvet cap that sat airily on his head, and a loose-fitting doublet of the same rich velvet encased his body. Such was Leonardo da Vinci, the Florentine, already known throughout Italy as poet, philosopher, painter, engineer, anatomist and sculptor.

Among the choristers from the Duomo, who thus invaded the refectory in the hope of seeing the master at work, was one who had not been there before—Galeazzo, sweetest and most boyish of the singers. The great picture came before him in its beauty, despite the scaffolding that partly concealed it. In the foreground was the long table around which were the excited disciples. In the exact center, vaguely suggested, was the unfinished figure of the Christ, his palms extended. He had just uttered the fateful words, "One of you shall betray me." In little groups the agitated disciples were asking, "Is it I?" In the background were green fields of Lombardy and a peaceful, winding river, which the art of the painter had put there to accentuate the turmoil in the hearts of the apostles.

The masterwork was incomplete in its two most important figures—the Christ and his betrayer. Judas sat in the dark, clutching a money bag, his face a black smear; and the Christ-head was represented only by a nimbus.

Galeazzo's eyes roved from end to end of the picture. There seemed something sinister in that dark blotch of pigment that covered the yet unpainted Judas-head. But in that golden nimbus at the center, over the gentle figure of Christ—what glory of feature, what sublime gentleness had the painter in mind to place there? What man so blameless in his thoughts, so pure in his life, that he could dare hope to be the model for the Christ-head?

Meditating thus, Galeazzo realized why the painter had left both figures unfinished. Truly, there was no man on earth worthy of the first honor, nor any living soul so black as to attain the evil distinction of being the Judas-model. Leonardo must perforce delve into the storehouse of his own mind to portray two such faces for the world to gaze upon. The young singer's eyes swept to the black smear. He thought of his lovely young wife, and the happiness of his own life, and was glad that no such sinister figure stalked the streets of Milan, to throw its evil shadow upon his happiness by its mere presence in the same city.

As he gazed, oblivious to his whispering companions, to the quiet figures of the two monks, to everything except the uncompleted masterpiece before him, he had the uncomfortable feeling that he was being watched. The dark unpainted Judas-head seemed exercising a baleful influence upon him. The feeling became so strong that he shivered, and raised his eyes.

Leonardo's gaze was resting upon his face, seeming to bore into his soul. The painter had been watching him thus for many minutes. Galeazzo let his glance fall, and a troubled presentiment took hold of him. Then Leonardo spoke, in a soft, musical voice. He had found in Galeazzo the model for his Christ-head.

Galeazzo could not believe his good fortune. He, the young cathedral singer of Milan, to be immortalized in this greatest of paintings! For it seemed inconceivable that there ever could be another painting as splendid as this, or another master as great as Leonardo. Gratefully he thanked the painter, and hurried home to break the wonderful news to his young wife. And Leonardo, mounting the scaffold, worked a short while on the gabardine of Judas, then hastened away from the convent to his colossal statue of the horse in the square before the ducal palace.

2

Galeazzo, in his joyous excitement, omitted the whistle with which he usually announced his approach. His wife gave a little shriek of dismay as he bounded into the room. The sound died away in a hysterical laugh.

"You frightened me, Galeazzo. Why did you not whistle, so that I could run to welcome you?"

Galeazzo became aware of a young man, standing awkwardly in the shadows of the ill-lighted room, clumsily fingering the jewelled hilt of his dagger. He was a handsome blade, rather effeminate in his beauty, with a slender, neatly twisted black mustache and a short beard that came hardly to the point of his chin.

"My cousin, Giovanni Malpierro," said Galeazzo's wife. "Giovanni, this is my Galeazzo, whom you have never seen."

The young man removed his fingers from the dagger-hilt. His white teeth flashed in a smile. Nervously he lifted one hand to twirl his mustache. His black eyes met the gray ones of Galeazzo, and fell uneasily.

"Giovanni?" asked Galeazzo. "Malpierro?"

"From Brescia," his wife explained. "Surely, Galeazzo, I have told you of my cousin, Giovanni Malpierro, from Brescia. He is the nephew of my Uncle Buoso. Do you remember now?"

"You are welcome, very welcome," said Galeazzo. "But in truth I took you for a southerner, for your skin is almost as dark as our duke's. You will stay and break bread with us, for nobody in Milan can cook like my Gianna."

He tilted her head and kissed her full on the lips, which was not his custom. She exchanged a look with him whom she had called Giovanni Malpierro.

"I must beg off this time," Giovanni hastened to reply. "I have a dear friend, Pietro Corni, who is expecting me, and I can refuse him nothing, even though," he added glibly, "it keeps me from my Cousin Gianna, whom I have not seen for two years, since before she was married."

"Well, I will not interpose," said Galeazzo, "especially since I have pleasant news for Gianna's ear alone. But we count on your company tomorrow."

So saying, he saw Giovanni to the door, and waved him adieu. Then he turned to Gianna and kissed her again, on the forehead, tenderly. She pouted.

"Galeazzo, why will you come like this, without warning me? You know how dearly I love to greet you, and today you bounded up the stairs like a wild beast, and were upon me before I could even smile."

"Gianna, my dearest," he answered, "it is because I was bursting with glad news. The great master Leonardo, the greatest painter since the world began, has chosen me for his Christ-head."

"Is that all?" asked Gianna. "Indeed I thought you were going to tell me that the duke had taken you under his protection, and you were to sing at the palace. But now I can have those blue slippers, and the ruby clasp for my bodice."

"Gianna, dearest, I will get you the slippers, but not the ruby clasp. For I have nothing, as you know, Gianna, except my cathedral pay, and what I have put away from the largess at the duke's ball."

"But will not the painter pay you?"

"Not a single soldo. But I am grateful beyond words that he has chosen me. I pose for him tomorrow."

Gianna's eyes opened wide in incredulity.

"But the duke?" she asked. "He has the painter under his protection. Surely the duke will give you something."

"No, my own, he will not. But no more of this now. Let us eat."

3

In the master's study Galeazzo roamed as in a fairyland. Half-finished heads were on the walls; strange, fabulous monsters fought; hideous faces laughed and leered from all corners of the room. Lying on a table was a pen-and-ink sketch of Bacio Bandini, the assassin, hanging from the gallows. Galeazzo shuddered, from horror of the subject more than of the picture. The criminal's hands were tied behind his back, and his face was in repose, as if he were merely sleeping.

Above the sketch were several lines of strange characters that puzzled Galeazzo. He studied them in mystified curiosity. They seemed to run from right to left. He took up the drawing and carried it to a small, burnished mirror that graced the sideboard Leonardo had carved for himself. A joyous chuckle escaped him as he held the sketch to the mirror, for he had solved the master's secret script. It was looking-glass writing, in which Leonardo had noted the date and circumstances of the hanging to mystify any prying eyes.

A soft voice trolled a snatch of song in the corridor, and the master entered his workshop. Galeazzo shamefacedly carried the sketch back to the table, crestfallen at being caught ferreting among the master's secrets. Leonardo laughed a mirthful, quiet laugh, so full of gentle humor and merriment that Galeazzo forgot his embarrassment and laughed too, but rather nervously.

"You remind me, Galeazzo," said Leonardo, "of a Florentine gamin, who climbed into my window and thought he was in a necromancer's den. So many terrible faces looked at him from the walls that he was quite beside himself with terror when I found him there. I told him funny stories, and sent him away with a picture of himself, as pleased as a peacock and as happy as a lark. But come, let us to work. I am in the working humor today, but I fear I have chased away the mood of revery in which you gazed at my painting yesterday."

He placed in Galeazzo's hand a notebook of sketches.

"Study the book," he said. "I want your eyes somewhat downcast, but not purposely so. Look at the pictures in the book."

As the master worked, he trolled again the song he had been singing when he entered the workshop. The mood seized Galeazzo, and he sang too, involuntarily. Then he remembered where he was, and sat with downcast eyes, gently humming from time to time. Leonardo caught a certain expression of the mouth, and encouraged him to hum some more.

They worked until Galeazzo began to weary. Then the master sent him home, and he walked rapidly through the streets, for Giovanni Malpierro was to be at dinner. Gianna came running to meet him as he whistled his approach, and they entered the house together.

With the beginning of the next week, Galeazzo went

with Leonardo to the convent of St. Mary of the Graces, and there the master began the head of Christ. He had studied the moods of the young singer, until he felt able to draw from them the expression of divine resignation and beatific peace that should shine from the features of Christ in the Cenacolo.

The picture was already the wonder of Italy, unfinished though it was. The sunlight seemed to break through the wall of the convent and flood the place where was to be the face of Christ. The painter's individuality had made even the hands of the disciples eloquent with meaning. Every gaze, every gesture, every line of the great painting carried the eyes of the beholder to that central nimbus.

Galeazzo could no more keep from breaking into song, while the master painted his head in place of the golden nimbus, than could the skylark, lifted up to heaven. He seemed no longer a mere chorister from the Duomo, but felt that he had taken on much of the nobility and tenderness of the Christ himself. The features grew and changed and gained in majesty under the slow, sure hands of the master, and Galeazzo thought of his young wife, Gianna, whom he loved more than life, and in the gratefulness of a full heart, he sang.

He went home, betimes, to find the dark-skinned Giovanni Malpierro with his Gianna. The young man, said Gianna, would stay in Milan longer, for he was trying, through friends, to gain a position in the duke's service, a position of trust that would pay him well. Giovanni gave him to understand that he was in the duke's favor, and that in a short time he would be a prosperous man. His cousin Gianna and her husband would share in his prosperity, he said. Galeazzo did not see the meaning looks they exchanged behind his back. Glad that Gianna had such pleasant comradeship, he was too happy in his love for her and his joy in Leonardo's painting to view their comradeship with eyes of suspicion.

4

The day came when the Christ-head was completed. Bathed in the soft sunlight of a Lombard springtime, Galeazzo saw himself idealized, the central figure of the master's painting. The Cenacolo was now finished except for the portentous spot of black that topped the Judas-figure. Galeazzo shuddered, as he had shuddered when he saw that smear for the first time, and as he had shuddered when he saw the sketch of the assassin in the master's workshop. In that minute he hoped that Leonardo might never complete the painting, and that the dark Judas might be forever without a counterpart in this world.

Leonardo let him gaze his fill. Then he addressed him cheerily, and invited him to his workshop.

"I have something for you, Galeazzo," said Leonardo, "that I think you will esteem, and keep always with you."

They walked rapidly through the streets, but the young singer fretted at what seemed to him a snail's pace. The master had a gift for him, and he was consumed with eagerness to know what it was. Why, then, did they not hurry? But Leonardo smiled at him, and gently rebuked him, and asked him to come often to see him and he would sketch him again.

They entered the workshop, and there the master gave to Galeazzo a porcelain medallion, hung on a slender silver chain. On it he had painted Galeazzo's head in the attitude of the Christ-head in the Cenacolo, and signed the token in the back-handed script that Galeazzo already knew how to decipher. Leonardo had made the porcelain himself, and baked the colors into it.

Galeazzo cried out, as delighted as a child. He thanked the master profusely, and would fain have kissed his hands, but Leonardo forbade and sent him away to show the miniature to the young wife whom he adored.

A group of jovial companions from the Duomo accosted Galeazzo as he passed through the street, and wanted him to drink with them. Impatiently he would have put them aside. He showed them the medallion, with the Christ-head—his own head—baked into the porcelain. He could not tarry, he told them, for he was burning with eagerness to show this treasure to Gianna, and perchance her cousin Giovanni Malpierro, who was a frequent visitor in his household.

A hoarse laugh greeted mention of Giovanni. The merry fellow who uttered it was plainly intoxicated. His companions tried to silence him with deprecating glances and shaking of heads, but he only laughed more obscenely than before.

Galeazzo seized him by the arm.

"Come now, Gian," he exclaimed. "What is behind all this ribald noise?"

Too much Lombardy wine had made Gian hilarious. He leered, and laughed again.

"You said, eh? Giovanni Malpierro? Ho, ho, ho!"

Galeazzo's face grew dark. He shook the drunken Gian.

"What do you mean? Giovanni Malpierro is my wife's cousin, from Brescia! Is there anything wrong about that? Speak up! Let me have the truth of this, or I will squeeze it out of your throat!"

He shook the now terrified and helpless Gian again, and let him fall into the street.

"Malpierro?"

Gian weakly strove to clamber to his feet.

"Yes, Malpierro! Giovanni Malpierro! What of him?"

Galeazzo's companions had never seen him aroused. But never before had any whisper involved his young wife Gianna, and a nameless frantic terror drove all other thoughts from his mind. Gianna unchaste? Gianna deceive him? It was unthinkable!

The drunken chorister succeeded in rising from the cobblestones, but Galeazzo seized him by the throat and forced him down into the filth of the gutter.

"Speak, dog!"

Gian's eyes rolled, and his face became purplish. The other choristers intervened, and dragged Galeazzo off.

"Come, Galeazzo, have you never suspected?"

Galeazzo shook himself free.

"Gianna? What of her? What of Giovanni Malpierro?"

"Galeazzo," said the chorister who had just spoken, "this man Giovanni is not Gianna's cousin, neither does he come from Brescia. He is no kin to you or yours, nor is his name Malpierro. Look well to your wife, Galeazzo."

The look of terror deepened in Galeazzo's eyes. His face became livid. He looked like one whose heart has been plucked out. Then suddenly he struck his informant in the mouth, and ran, frantically, wildly, clutching the miniature to his breast. He bounded up the steps of his home and burst into the house, out of breath, pale from fear.

"Gianna!" he called. "Gianna! Gianna! Gianna!"

Gianna did not answer. Galeazzo rushed through the

rooms like a maddened bull. In the bedroom he stood for a minute like a stone statue, then knelt beside the bed and sobbed like one in purgatory. For Gianna had gone. She had left only the simple dress in which she had performed her household tasks. The oaken chest was burst open, and she had taken even the coins he had saved from the duke's largess, the night he sang at the palace.

The whirlwind in his thoughts cleared somewhat, and he knelt beside the bed and prayed to the Virgin. He clasped his hands together, and cried out in his pain. Why should he, who had been so happy, be thus thrust into hell?

He turned the medallion tenderly in his hands. It was all that was left to him, now that Gianna was gone. The picture of the Christ-head, tranquil, resigned, full of peace unspeakable! Surely he, Galeazzo, had never looked like that! And yet here was the proof, in the calm, beatific features of the Christ-face in his hand.

He crossed the room, and looked at himself in the metal mirror that Gianna had kept so bright. He hardly recognized himself. What wildness in his eyes! What terror! And yet it was the same face as that on the porcelain medallion. The little oval seemed to promise that he should again be the happy, tranquil man he had been, though his heart was leaden and his hopes were dead. Despairingly he put the silver chain about his neck, and the master's amulet hung below his throat.

5

Gianna walked along cautiously, somewhat furtively, in the gathering dusk, notwithstanding that she did not see the figure of her husband. Galeazzo followed at a little distance, like a cat stalking a bird, fearful lest she should fly and avoid him. He skulked in doorways, and ran from one to another, silently, always keeping the object of his pursuit in sight.

He slunk into hiding as Gianna stopped. She searched the street on all sides, then suddenly entered one of the doorways. Galeazzo stood for a minute undecided. His blood raced like a mill-wheel, for he had found Gianna's hiding-place. And with her, doubtless, was Giovanni Malpierro, the dark-skinned betrayer of his hospitality.

Galeazzo leapt across the street, and dashed up the narrow stairway. He broke into the room like a hurricane. Gianna shrieked, once, and backed against the wall. She looked very white and frightened, and shot an imploring glance at her husband. Her chin trembled, and her eyelids fluttered.

Galeazzo stood with one hand on the latch, breathing hard, and looking at Gianna. How lovely she was! So delicate, so beautiful, so affectionate! Could it be she who had shattered his happiness and thus basely plunged him into the fires that were eating his brain and his heart? He would plead with her. He would ask her to go back with him. They would live happily together, and he would forgive. Who could not forgive his Gianna? It was Giovanni who was to blame. On Giovanni alone would his vengeance fall.

"Gianna!"

His voice sounded thin and far away, as if it issued from some other throat than his own. He scarcely recognized it. But its effect on Gianna was magical. Her fear vanished, and her voice rang out defiantly.

"What do you want? Why do you follow me?"

Galeazzo was on his knees in an instant.

"Gianna! Gianna! Come back to me! I love you, Gianna! I will forgive! Only come back to me!"

Gianna frowned, and bit her lip.

"You forgive? I am the one who should forgive, for it is you who have brought this about!"

Galeazzo seized the hem of her skirt, and pressed it to his lips.

"Gianna! Why has this happened? Say you love me, Gianna, as I love you! You must say that you love me, Gianna! Think of the past!"

"Yes, fool, I think of the past!" Gianna burst out, in a rage. "I think of the many months I spent with you, whom I despise, weakling, ninny that you are! I did love you, once, or thought I did; but that is all past, long ago. You and your contemptible goodness! I want a man I can love with all my body and soul, and not a goody-goody weakling who sings in the choir!"

The words cut like a knife. Galeazzo rose to his feet. His tongue had turned to ashes in his mouth. He felt his senses reeling.

"But I love you, Gianna!"

"Love me?" She laughed, hoarsely, mockingly. "Love me? You don't know what love is. Love is passion! Love is fire! Love is the meeting of souls that burn with longing! You in love?"

She laughed a little, mirthless laugh. And then her scorn blazed out with consuming heat, and lashed her husband, as he leaned against the wall, very pale and faint.

"You have dragged me through hell! I have cursed you every day and every night, almost since the day we were married! Oh, how I have hated you, with your woman's face and your silly little affection that you call love!"

She stamped her foot, and her voice rose shrilly.

"Leave me, do you hear? Giovanni will be here, and he will tear you limb from limb! I never truly loved you, and I hate you now! I hate you!"

She shook her fist in his face, and screamed into his ear.

"I hate you, Galeazzo! Do you hear?"

He threw his arms about her, and pressed his lips desperately against her mouth. She fought him off, and tore his face with her nails.

"I hate you!" she shrilled. "Now go, before it is too late."

Too late? Giovanni was coming, had she said? She wanted to get rid of him, then, because Giovanni was coming? These thoughts rushed like evil phantoms across his dazed brain, and wrought in him a fury. Gianna clawed his lips with her nails, and the taste of blood was in his mouth. He struck out madly, blindly. His clenched fist smote her on the breast, over the heart. She struggled for breath, convulsively, and uttered a little, stifled cry, then crumpled and sank to the floor.

Galeazzo bent over her, and shook her by the shoulders. She did not move. He put his ear to her heart. There was no sign of pulse. He chafed her hands, and covered her face with kisses. The whirlwind in his thoughts, the horror in his heart, the unutterable dread that gnawed at the pit of his stomach, were combining into one terrible cry for vengeance on the man that had wrought this ruin in his life. Gianna was dead! And he, Galeazzo, was her murderer!

Whose step was this ascending the stair, with stealthy, cat-like tread? Had not Gianna been expecting Giovanni? In a moment her seducer would stand within the room.

Stung with horror at his deed, mad with anger at him who had caused it, Galeazzo sprang noiselessly behind the door, and brandished a chair over his head. The door opened, and Giovanni entered the room. The chair came down upon his head with crushing force, and stretched him on the floor beside Gianna.

Every tongue of light from the windows of comfortable homes seemed an accusing finger as Galeazzo fled through the dark streets. He crept by in the shadows, to the safe haven of darkness, then ran desperately through the night until halted by another shaft of light. Fear clutched him tightly, choking him. Nameless terrors surrounded him. In each dark corner he fancied he saw her whom he had killed. He longed for light, yet shrank from it like a ghost.

His deed must have been discovered before now. Surely some one had heard Gianna shriek, and recognized his name as she spat out her taunts, before he struck her down! Surely Giovanni's heavy fall had not been unnoticed! It had seemed to shake the house. Even now they must be hunting him. Again he fancied he saw Gianna in the gloom, white-faced and scared as when he confronted her a few short hours before. He stopped short, and a strange trembling came upon him. But approaching footsteps sent him flying past the dreadful spot. The panic dread of capture scourged him forward.

He could not return, and he knew not where to flee. He dared not even confess himself. The thought that even the sanctuary of religion was denied to him made his whirling brain sick, and he fell, striking his head on the sharp cobbles of the street.

He was walking with Gianna, he thought, in the green fields in spring-time. His brain was on fire with love. Intoxicated by her alluring beauty, he threw his arms around her, and hotly kissed her eyes, her throat, her brow, her lips. She struggled against him, gently, then yielded to him. Her soft arms crept around his neck. He was living over again the great day of his life. But now she melted from his grasp, and other arms were about his neck, as he lay on the cobblestones. Some one was rolling him over. The hard reality of life laid its soiling hands upon him, and he groaned, and sat up. Fear of the duke's officers was strong within him, but it was only a poor thief that was searching him.

"Hide me!" Galeazzo begged. "Take me away where no one can ever find me!"

"*Va!*" said the thief, and spurned him with his foot.

Galeazzo sprang up. His many wrongs rushed hotly through his brain. He delivered a sturdy blow and knocked the fellow down.

"Lead me to your den, to your companions, or by all that's holy, I will murder you!"

He spat the words out through clenched teeth. One look at the anger-maddened face, and the thief no longer thought of refusing. Plainly he was in the hands of a madman. He rose from the dust and carefully examined himself. Then he motioned Galeazzo to follow, and slunk silently away.

The young singer overtook him and kept abreast of him, and they wandered off together. Not a word passed between them. But as they turned out of the narrow street, a burst of light from the rising sun flooded the city with silver, and the song of a shoemaker at work floated sweetly up from the neighboring street. The city was resuming its customary habits.

Galeazzo followed his unwilling guide down a dismal

labyrinth into a dirty room, and threw himself wearily upon a pallet of straw. For him had begun a new and strange existence, and his old life was irrevocably closed.

6

The swirl of carnival filled the streets with singing, laughing, shouting throngs. The Duke Lodovico was marrying Beatrice d'Este, and this auspicious union was the occasion of a joyous fête, in which the whole city joined. Happy, joyous, carefree, Milan gave itself up to rejoicing. Showers of confetti filled the air. Huge, multicolored lanterns were carried high upreared, and long streamers shot over the crowds. Groups of youths ran through the streets kissing the girls, and many an unwilling old crab was forced to drink the health of the duke and his bride in the sourest of sour chianti because he objected to being tripped up by the heels. The crowd gathered thickly about the horse of the duke, as he proceeded toward the Duomo, preceded by mounted men-at-arms and followed by the notables of Milan. He spoke a word from time to time to his chamberlain, who thereupon reached into a well-filled purse and scattered small silver coins among the crowd. Then was laughter, indeed, and gay shouts, and a wild scrambling to pick up the trophies.

Thieves worked among the throngs, for there were rich purses to pick that night. As the horses cavorted, and the long line moved slowly past, one of the boldest of the thieves attached himself to the vicinity of a stately, bearded man, dressed for the fête in green silk doublet and parti-colored tights, with slashed trunks that showed green and yellow as he walked. The man wore a strange wallet attached to his girdle, richly wrought in curious little figures and strange monsters and laughing heads, curiously tinted in contrasting tones. The wallet was a find worth having, for it was made by him who wore it, Leonardo da Vinci. The thief watched his opportunity and cut it from its moorings, only to find it fastened by a silver chain. He wrenched this free and shoved his way rapidly through the crowd, darting a glance over his shoulder. His eyes met those of Leonardo in a startled look of recognition, and he fled from the place as if it were accursed.

Leonardo's holiday mood vanished, and a somber musing fell upon him, for the face of the thief had struck some strange chord of memory. He fell to thinking of the Cenacolo in the refectory of St. Mary of the Graces, and a shadow gathered darkly on his brow, accentuating the lines that were already beginning to mark his face with the disillusionments of his life in Milan.

The men-at-arms and the notables of Milan had passed by, and the crowd had thinned. Lost in his musings, Leonardo took no note of the youths that ran shouting on both sides of him, until they caught him about the ankles with a long rope and spilled him into the filth of the street. He darted upon them a look so sour, so fierce, that they hustled him away to a wine-shop to make him buy drinks for them all. But his wallet was gone, and he had not a soldo on his person. They forced him to gulp down a bitter, vinegarish wine, and mocked his grimaces as he drank it. Then he wandered the streets, restless and perturbed from the evil presentiments of his mood, and deeply troubled by thoughts he could not explain.

The Duke Lodovico, visiting the convent of St. Mary of the Graces to see what additional gifts his bounty could provide, stopped before the great mural of Leonardo and gazed with ill-concealed displeasure at the unfinished figure of Judas and the sinister blot that represented the head. The prior took this occasion to voice his complaint against Leonardo.

"Sire," he said, "the great painter sits sometimes a whole morning in contemplation of the Cenacolo without so much as approaching the scaffolding. At other times he makes but two or three strokes with his brush and hurries away. And here is the Cenacolo, my lord, with the Judas incomplete, while Montorfano's painting, begun a scant six months ago, is already finished and perfect. I have complained in vain to Master Leonardo. Can you not use your good offices with this Florentine, my lord?"

Irritation showed for a fleeting instant in Leonardo's face. But immediately he masked his feelings, and gave ear to the prior's complaint with an air of lofty condescension. Lodovico looked grave, for the prior had expressed the thought the duke himself was thinking.

"I have asked for greater speed," said the duke. "You have vouchsafed no explanation. For years the picture has been like this, with no perceptible change. The black splotch where the Judas-head should be remains a reproach to the convent. Select your Judas, Master Leonardo, and bring your picture to completion."

Leonardo bowed low.

"My lord, it is a deep sorrow to me that the picture is as you see it," he said. "But the complaints of the prior are unjust, for I work just as truly in these hours that I spend in contemplation as when I actually have the brushes in my hand. There is the time when one builds his ideas, and there is also the time when one brings them into reality with his paints. I have been unable to find any face so base that I could use it as the model for the Judas. But if my lord insists, I will delay no longer. I can always fall back on the prior for my model; and indeed his head will not go badly in place of that black smear."

The duke smiled paternally, as at the sally of some child.

From that day Leonardo forsook his paintings and his sculpturing until he should find his Judas-head. He wandered into low dens of vice, and haunts of crime. Many evil faces he saw, but not evil enough. He demanded perfection in evil. No ordinary head could represent the betrayer of Christ. In the last extremity he could fall back on his imagination, but he continued the search longer, to find a living model for the face that, next to Christ himself, should be the most important in the whole great picture.

He appealed to Duke Lodovico for permission to seek in the prisons, and he searched the dungeons, and the cells occupied by prisoners awaiting trial. Much of evil he saw, and many faces that were marked with patient resignation. Some were sullen, others stolid. Some had been cleansed by suffering, and others had been hardened. But only in the last cell of all did he find a face so lost to good impulses that it could fittingly represent the face of Judas.

The occupant of the cell was a felon condemned to die. He had treacherously murdered two companions in crime for their share of plunder. He was still a young man, but his face was old in evil. The features were hard, and the furtive, steely eyes were the perfect expression of cruelty and treachery. The face was devoid of all soulful qualities, and evil sat on his countenance like a dark cloud.

Leonardo had found his Judas. Satisfied at last, yet secretly chagrined that he could not now use the head of the prior, he ordered the criminal taken to the convent of St. Mary of the Graces.

Wrathfully the felon glared at the painter who had obtained for him this brief reprieve. He leered at his guards. His tongue was silent, but the sullen fires of his hate blazed out unconcealed as he transfixed the Christ-head and the Judas with his terrible gray eyes.

The man's eyes troubled Leonardo, for they reminded him of something he had seen. He pondered as he painted; then suddenly the picture of that night of carnival came before him, and he remembered the stolen wallet and the startled glance of the thief as their eyes met. The Judas was the thief who had robbed him.

He painted rapidly, for the guile and craftiness of the face disturbed his calm. He felt the felon's eyes fixed upon him, and he wished the man gone. The prior came in as he painted, and rubbed his hands in satisfaction at seeing another head than his own in the place of the betrayer. The felon turned upon him a look so charged with poison that the prior's chuckle died in his throat. He stammered out a few words to Leonardo, and removed himself from the chamber.

The Judas-head was soon finished, and the model was returned to his felon's cell. The prison authorities laid violent hands upon him, and twisted a rope about his neck, in accordance with the sentence of the law. When the law was satisfied, they lowered the body and searched it.

Around the neck of the dead criminal, hanging on a

silver chain, was a small porcelain medallion that bore the picture of a handsome young man, with eyes downcast in quiet resignation. Strange characters ran from right to left on the medallion. The prisonmaster recognized these as the secret script of the painter Leonardo, and he carried his find to the master.

Deeply agitated, Leonardo looked long at the face on the medallion. He turned it in his hands and pondered the features, as if he sought from that little oval the answer to some tremendous problem that vexed him. At length he motioned the prisonmaster into the convent, and they turned aside into a small room where was a mirror. With fingers that trembled, he held the porcelain medallion before this mirror, that the prisonmaster might read therein the strange characters that had puzzled him.

Under the youthful face were written these words:

"To Galeazzo, in whose joyous features I have seen the image of the Christ.—Leonardo da Vinci."

WHAT'S IN A NAME?

Judge, March 5th 1921

Josiah Brush was a travelling man,
  Who travelled the briny main;
He was "Mr. Brush" in England,
  And "Señor Brush" in Spain;
The Frenchmen called him "Monsieur Brush,"
  But the Germans were his bane,
For they always called him "Herr Brush,"
  Which filled his soul with pain.

TWO CROWS

Weird Tales, January 1925

Two crows flapped over dismally
(So wearily, so drearily)
To the blackened limb of a blasted tree;
The shells flew screaming overhead,
And the field was covered thick with dead—
The earth reeked with its dead.

One crow lamented to his mate
(So wearily, so drearily) :
"How long, how long must we now wait
For the taste of food that was so good
Before the shrapnel shattered the wood
And loaded the ground with dead?

"The odor sweet of dying men"
(Lamented he so drearily),
"How strangely pleasant was it when
I sensed it first with ravished breath!
But I am sated, and sick to death,
And would fain lie yon with the dead."

A shell came moaning through the air
(So drearily, so eerily)
And burst where the crows were plaining there;
It shivered the wreck of the blasted tree,
And bits of crow fell bloodily
Among the tangled dead.

THE DARK POOL

Weird Tales, April 1925

It lies beneath a sunless sky,
   Deep in the entrails of a bog:
Gnarled willows hide it, lifting high
   Their tortured arms; and never frog,
Nor newt, nor toad, nor dragonfly
   Dare come within its deadly fog.

For evil spirits there are bound
   Within its slime: an impious rune
They chant, nor is there other sound
   But wicked whispers, out of tune,
As un-dead *things* that there lie drowned
   Obscenely mutter to the moon.

The nightshade petals in its dank
   And fetid vapors darkly bloom;
Black orchids on its silent bank
   Insinuate a sick perfume;
And from its depths ooze up the rank
   And gassy stenches of the tomb.

For potencies of witchcraft fell
   Are buried in its slimy bed,
And deathly blasphemies that well
   And bubble up with grisly dread.
From *things* that in its waters dwell—
   From *things* that died, but are not dead.

THE DEATH ANGEL

Weird Tales, September 1925

We struggled in the waves, and I was ware
Of a strange presence moving by my side,
More beautiful than dawn, and dreamy-eyed,
Who half enmesht me with her falling hair,
Blacker than night, yet thousandfold more fair;
And with the siren-voice of dreams she cried:
"Forbear to struggle more, but gently slide
Into my arms: new rapture waits thee there."

To that soft plea I would have yielded then,
But tender voices cried into my ear,
And then the sobs of loved ones I could hear;
And so I turned, and fought the waves again.
My comrade from my side she reft away:
I entered into night, he into day.

THE EVENING STAR

Weird Tales, March 1926

The ruddy sun has fled to west, and his diurnal flight
Has reft away the shining day, and given us the night;
The woods are still, and on the hill is dying fast the
light.

With cheerful gleam now trembles forth a radiance in
the sky,
Shines from afar the evening star, resplendent in the
sky;
With love aglow, on Earth below she beams with
lustrous eye.

Above the trees, above the hills, above the western
sea,
Far, far above, the star of love moves on in ecstasy,
And the trembling light of the eye of night descends
like balm to me.

The pallid moon is not so bright, and she weeps in
her throne on high;
She is not so bright as the gorgeous light of that
darling of the sky,
As the blue, blue light of the eye of night, where it
sparkles across the sky.

The silver stars are now aglow, and they twinkle
ceaselessly;

Stationed on high, they throng the sky, a splendid
    company,
An escort throng, the whole night long, afloat in a
    purple sea.

And I tread no longer the dusky Earth, I am floating
    up there in the sky;
I am floating above with the star that I love, in the
    violet deeps of the sky;
Far, far above, in the realms of love, in the depths of
    the purple sky.

SELF-PORTRAIT

Fantasy Magazine, April 1935

The editor's a gloomy guy, who fusses, fumes and
frets;
He puts in all his cheerless life expressing his regrets,
And you should see the things he sees when perched
upon his Eyrie;
The shuddering shapes and eldritch forms, and dim
things out of Faerie.
Around the eaves the spiders weave their webs, and
bat-things flutter,
While vampires drear breathe in his ear of thoughts
too wild to utter.
For music he hears werewolves howl all night to
serenade him;
This symphony cacophonous a shivering wreck has
made him.
Ah, look! what slithering shapes are these that on his
desk are crawling?
Their red eyes fix upon his throat with avid lust
appalling,
Till (just between ourselves, you know) he scarce can
keep from bawling.
With obscene grins and fleshless chins tall skeletons
do mock him,
Till he's reduced to a quivering pulp in fear that one
might sock him.
Stone wyverns guard the adytum of darkness where
he labors;

Ghosts fly about in a grisly rout, and witches beat
   their tabors.
A murdered lich stands sentinel beside the office
   portal—
A zombie he, undead, yet dead; immortal, and yet
   mortal.
So all the day and all the night the editor gives battle
To spooks and warlocks, wizards, snakes, until his
   jawbones rattle.
So come, ye bards and raconteurs, send him your
   stories creepy;
Be sure they're weird, for if they're not, they'll merely
   make him sleepy;
Stories that bite as well as bark, convincing yarns that
   floor him—
These are, to him, both food and drink; all other kinds
   just bore him.

AFTER TWO NIGHTS OF THE EAR-ACHE

Weird Tales, October 1937

Most gentle Sleep! Two nights I wooed in vain;
Thou wouldst not come to banish racking pain:
For what is Sleep but Life in stone bound fast?
Oblivion of the Present, Future, Past.

WHO NEVER ATE WITH TEARS HIS BREAD

The World's Great Religious Poetry, ed. Caroline Miles Hill, 1924[*]

Who never ate with tears his bread,
Who never through the troubled hours
Weeping sad upon his bed,
He knows ye not, ye heavenly powers.

Ye lead us into life amain,
Ye let the poor with guilt be weighted,
And then ye give him o'er to pain,
For guilt must all be compensated.

[*] Translated by Farnsworth Wright from the German of Goethe.

SONG OF THE BROTHERS OF MERCY

Weird Tales, December 1926[*]

With rapid pace on strideth Death;
   No breathing spell to man is given:
Midway the course Death stops his breath,
   And sends him to his God unshriven;
And whether he's prepared or no,
Each man before his Judge must go.

[*]Translated (as by Francis Hard), from the German of Friedrich von Schiller.

Best wishes, yours sincerely,

Wright

www.ingramcontent.com/pod-product-compliance
Lightning Source LLC
Chambersburg PA
CBHW070633170726
48291CB00003B/1000